I0663593

Power of Truth

Poweress Series Book 2

By Minniel Douglas

Dedication:

To my Mommie, who taught me at a young age, it was ok to be authentic, unique, and exactly who God created me to be. Thank you for teaching me that it is ok to live life at the beat of my own drum and for showing me that living this way is the most fulfilling way to live.

To my Husband, who is always in my corner, showing me the bigger picture when tunnel vision wants to set in. Thank you for showing me that boldness in truth is well worth the reward even though it is a battle to live out.

Thank you both for being the wonderful people that God created you to be in the world, in our family, and in my life. Love you forever and always.

Copyright

Note:

This title is a standalone; however, please take a moment and read the other titles in the series. This title is also for adults only. It contains some themes, actions, and language that may be offensive to some.

Table of Contents

Chapter 1: Trina

"OH Yess!! Just like that! Just a little harder! Oh, my Gaud, you don't know how long it has been since someone has done it right," I moan excitedly.

"Has anyone ever rotated left?" Jack questions.

"Left, oh is that left. Yess, rotate! Rotate! Oh Yess!! That's it! That's it!! Oh, my Gaud, you are the best I've ever had." I sigh with relief and turn to look him in his eyes. He winks at me and says, "Happy to be of service. We aim to please."

He gets off me and uses the discarded towel to wipe off my back. For him to be such a muscular dude, it is weird how gentle he is right now compared to a few minutes ago.

"Trina, I can't believe that is the best massage you have ever had. Where do you want me to put this towel?"

"You can put it in the washroom. The last door on the right." I state as I get up and put back on my bra and top. To be honest, when we agreed to come to my house after our mutual friends, my best friend and his best friend are married, kicked us out because they got tired of our sexual tension; I really thought it was going to be a one-night stand. You know, get loved down by a fine man and then move on to the next, but on the drive to my place, my back started hurting from an old dance injury. I usually get massages like twice a week because if I don't, the muscle tends to bunch, especially if I haven't been to dance. The last two months have been a whole mess. So, no, I haven't had any fun, just work and work, and more work. I work as a commercial realtor for Lord & Son Inc, a commercial real estate firm. It's funny because my friends really think I am a fly-by-night kind of girl. I won't lie before two years ago, I switched jobs every 2-3 years. Now I think I have finally found something I like to do. I get to sell amazing commercial properties and get paid to travel the world to do it.

Anyway, back to Jack, his name is Jackson, we were coming to my place, and when I told him about my back, he told me he was a certified massage therapist. Now really, what ex-air force pilot you know used to give massages. So, I clowned him, and he said OK, let me show you. The next thing I know, we are on my bed with me topless and him working out kinks that no massage therapist has ever been able to work out. When I tell you, it felt like heaven, almost as good as an orgasm, almost.

"Trina, can I have a macaroon?" Jack is yelling from the kitchen.

"Oh, so you just all comfortable in my spot, now?"

"Well, I mean, I did put in work. The least you could do is give a brotha a macaroon."

Laughing as I enter the kitchen and take a seat on one of the barstools, "Whatever! You can have two, but that's it."

"Yes, Ma'am," he laughs. As I watch him pick out his macaroons, I take a moment to really check him out. Usually, we are around friends, and as much as I don't mind them knowing, I'm interested in someone. I don't really like them seeing me on the prowl.

Jackson is at least 6'1" as he is much taller than my 5' 6" frame. He is the color of pure honey, which has been golden and toasted to perfection. His voice is smooth and deep like molasses. His nice strong arms look like they could lift you high, and his muscular thighs look to have the perfect strength to hold you steady as he drills into you and pushes you against the wall. As I watch him take a bite of one of the macaroons, I let my eyes wander to his strong jawline covered in a nicely trimmed soft beard. I watch as his plump brownish pink lips open and then engulf the entire macaroon. I hear him moan in appreciation for the baked goodness that it is. Then I allow my eyes to ascend to his well-shaped nose, not pointy but not wide, and when I get to those caramel pools of intensity that are his eyes, I realize I have been caught red-handed checking him out in slow detail. He smiles at me and picks up his second macaroon, and then walks over to me. He places the macaroon right in front of my mouth. I lick my lips slowly and watch as his eyes dart down to my mouth and he licks his lips. I ever so slowly take a bite of the chocolate chip macaroon that happens to be my favorite. When I moan in response, I see him adjust himself slightly. He looks into my eyes, and the caramel pools now appear black as night, and before I know it, he has come around the bar and walked right between my legs. He picks me up and places me on top of the bar.

He stares at me as if he is waiting for me to make my move. The truth is I don't back down from a challenge, so make my move I do. I pull him closer to me and open my legs wider to get closer access, and then I put my arms around his neck and tug him into me. He kisses me slowly and firmly, allowing me to fill the pressure of him from my mouth to the apex of my thighs. Then he slides his tongue along my lower lip, asking for access into my mouth. I grant his request. I open my mouth and receive his tongue; the kiss kicks up times 10. His arms have wrapped around me, and my hands are running from his neck up through his curly mane. His hair feels as soft as I always thought it would. He is thoroughly exploring my mouth, and our tongues are dancing with a rhythm that is all their own. Our tongues slide across each other, back and forward, twist and slide, and then he sucks in my bottom lip, and I take the opportunity to suck his plump top lip. I cannot help but let out a moan. Eventually, we both lean back and stare into each other's eyes with smiles on our faces. I always knew this man would be a good kisser.

Chapter 2: Trina

I pick up the rest of the macaroon on the bar and put it in my mouth and start chewing. He just watches me intently. I wait. I am in no rush. Eventually, he says, "Trina, what are we doing?"

"Whatchu wanta do Jackson?" He smirks at me, calling him his full name and not the nickname that everyone uses.

"What I wanta do is, You." He states bluntly.

"Then do that."

Before I get the statement out of my mouth good, he is picking me up and taking me to my bedroom. When he puts me on my bed, I remove my shirt, and he follows suit. Then I remove my pants he follows suit. Then he begins to remove his boxers. When I go to do the same, he shakes his head no. So, I stop. When he has pulled his boxers all the way down, I look down, and his dick is calling my name. He is wide and long with a chocolate and caramel base and smooth brown head. He curves up ever so slightly, exposing his thick veins. I moan, just looking at him, well, his dick, that is. I love dicks. I know it's weird, but I do. I love how they look, how they feel, and how they taste. It's a problem, really. Jack's dick is one of the most impressive dicks I have seen, and I am so ready for this ride. When I meet his eyes, I see that cocky dude who is constantly checking me out. He smirks at me and says, "You like what you see?"

Licking my lips, "Absolutely." With that, he walks over to me and unlatches my bra, and he watches with what appears to be excitement as my 36DDs fall forward. He leans in and takes one into his mouth, and I love every stroke of his tongue around my nipple. Then he goes to pull down my panties, and his phone vibrates from his pants on the floor. He ignores it and continues to pull my panties down my legs. But then his phone buzzes two more times. He groans, and his head falls forward.

"I'm sorry about this. Let me go silence it."

"Maybe you should check to see who it is? It could be one of your many hoes."

"Hoes? Really, that's what you think?" He says as he walks to his pants.

"Naw, if that's what I thought, you wouldn't be here."

"Exactly," he states as he pulls his phone out of his pants pocket.

I watch as he reads the text messages, and a frown begins to form on his face. The more he reads, the angrier he seems to get. Then he starts to put his clothes back on. I'm sorry what the world is what I am screaming in my head. I get up and put on a robe as he puts on his pants and makes a call. All he says is, "I'm on the way."

He pulls on his shirt and then finally looks my way. I am really about to let him have it. Then I look into those pools of caramel, and he says, "Sorry about this, Trina, but it's my Moms. I got to go."

"Is your Mom ok?"

"Yeah, it's a long story. Anyway, listen, I will make good on what I started. You got my word on that." He tells me with a smirk.

I smile and lean in and hug him, and I lick his ear and say, "I will hold you to that."

"Do that." With that, he squeezes me tight, and we head to the door.

As I open the door so he can leave my loft, "Tell your Mom I said hi and let me know if I can help in any way."

He smiles at me and says, "Bet." With that, he is headed to the elevator and headed out.

****

After he leaves, I grab a glass of wine and sit on the couch. I start to think about the first time I met his mother at Lyric and Ezekiel's wedding; those are our mutual friends. He was the best man, and I was one of the bridesmaids.

"Gurl, that man is too fine. Are you sure it would be wrong of me to be one of those bridesmaids who jump the best man? I mean, I can pretend I was drunk and don't remember, however by the way those pants are fitting, I am pretty sure I would not forget any part of a night with him." I explain to Erica.

"Gurl, no!! We will have to see him. He is Eze's best friend. There is no way that will not come back to bite you. Pinky swear you will find someone else to be your next rendezvous?"

"Man, Liza, you feel the same way?"

"Yes."

"You don't have to say it like that." Looking at my two best friends with their pinkies out, ready for me to promise. I take a long breath, and then I pinky promise. The reception processional music begins, and when I walk down the aisle, I watch as Jackson's eyes roam my whole body. When our eyes meet, he gives me a cocky wink and a sexy smirk.

This behavior has been the norm for us since we met, and tonight is no different. Every time I look up, I find Jackson ready to give me a cocky wink and a sexy smirk, but not once does he make a move. It's like he had to pinky promise too. After returning his smirk with one of my own, I turn around and walk to the nearby table. The shoes Lyric picked for us are super cute, but they hurt something fierce. As I am taking off my shoes, an older woman comes and sits right next to me. She has some of the most mesmerizing caramel eyes that I have ever seen.

"Hello, Sweets. Those shoes finally catchin' up with cha?" Her voice is filled with humor and has a little bit of shake that tells you her age.

"Yes, Ma'am."

"Well, I noticed you dancin'. You got nice moves. Are you a dancer?"

"I used to be. Injuries and age took me out of the game."

"Well, some Epson salt and regular massages can go a long way to keepin' you movin'. Oh, and don't forget a little peppermint and heat."

"You sound like you used to dance."

"Oh, I did. A long time ago. My moves were more ballet and jazz, though."

"It is always nice to meet a fellow dancer, and thanks for the tips. I will try the regular massages. I haven't done that yet." *I smiled at her, and she returned the favor.*

"Hey there, hot mama. You ready to cut a rug with me?" *That was the voice of none other than Jackson. I was thinking it was about time, but then when I looked around, he was talking to the older woman sitting next to me.*

"Hey Trina, you don't mind if I steal my Moms for a sec. They bout to play our jam." *His mom?*

I looked at her just as she said, "Me and Trina, is it?"

"Yes. Ma'am"

"We were just getting acquainted. I mean, I noticed you seem not to be able to keep your eyes off her, so I minus well meet her." *She starts to laugh at the look of shock on Jack's face. I giggle to myself.*

"Moms, really? That's what we doin today?'

"Ain't no time like the present, boy."

Jack shakes his head. I tell them, "Y'all should go dance. The song just changed."

He looks my way and smiles that delicious 10-watt perfect teeth dimpled smile.

"Oh, Jack, why don't you finally go dance with Trina? You minus well touch what you have been lookin' at."

"Moms, have you been drinkin'? Trina, she is usually not this bad."

That night was beautiful. Later that night, I talked to Ms. Kathy, Jackson's mom, and we exchanged phone numbers. Over the past five years, we have hosted multiple dance camps and workshops together. Come to find out, she taught dance too. She has become my mentor in some ways. She is very insightful and hilarious. That makes me think about what she would have to say if something happened between me and Jack. Would she turn all nobody is good enough for my son, or would she embrace me?

The truth is I never actually meet the mothers of the men I date. I usually sleep with them, and then we hang out for about 2-3months, and then I am on to the next. That is the reason my friends didn't want me messing with Jack. But the truth is what we started was bound to happen with how often we all hang out. The sexual chemistry has always been there, and neither of us seems to be the kind that needs to settle down.

I get up to get myself some more wine, and it dawns me, why am I even thinking about this? Usually, I hit it and move on. Why am I taking a pause now that we started but are not finished? I drink my wine and shoot Jackson a quick text.

Hey, how is your mom?

Hey fine. I had to kick this dude Trevor out of her house, but she good now.

45-year-old Trevor? Her landscaper?

Yep, the one and only. Wait, did you know this was a thing.

I kinda guessed based on how she was talking.

Man, we gone talk. Got my mom's out here being a panther.

That's her, not me. LOL

With that, I lay down and go to sleep. Today has been a weird day.

Chapter 3: Trina

I have in my Airpod pros in transparent mode, and I am dancing to "Type a Way" by Eric Bellinger. I woke up horny and in the mood to bake. Baking is my secret pastime; not even my besties know I do it. Usually, I just let them think I bought whatever desserts I bring around. I have more macaroons in the oven, and I am slow whining and grinding with my Swiffer jet as I mop the floor. I do a few leg lifts and leaps, and then I lap dance on the couch, picturing Jackson underneath me. I am in the middle of giving my imaginary partner a nice grind to his crotch when I hear a knock at the door. I turn off the music and head to the door and look through the peephole. I don't know who it could be since it is 8am on a Saturday, and none of my friends would come over at this time of the morning.

I look out the peephole and see a bouquet from edible arrangements. I open the door to sign for my delivery, but then I realize that the delivery guy is Jackson.

"Boy, what you are doing here this early?"

"Apologizing for leaving."

"You didn't have to do that. Moms comes first. I get it." I say as I let him into the loft.

"Trina, what is that smell? It smells delicious."

"It's me." I laugh.

He steps into my space and gives me that cocky stare. He deepens his voice to that radio after dark tone and says, "Sweetheart, I am sure you smell delicious, but that smells like baked goods."

I smile up at him. I want to say all kinds of dirty things, especially since I was just lap dancing to an imaginary version of him, but instead, I reply, "I made more macaroons. I may have finished the box for breakfast." I laugh.

"Wait, you made those macaroons?"

"Yeah," I say shyly.

"Girl, you been holding out. What else can you cook?"

"I don't really cook, sorry. I just bake. I bake literally everything."

"Seriously?" He sounds shocked.

"Oh, come on. Is it really that surprising? I literally bring a dessert to everything." I say, putting my hands on my hips.

"That's true. I guess it just shows there is so much we don't know about each other." With that, he sits at my bar. He looks a little sad compared to normal. I get some plates and come and sit next to him. I open the edible arrangement, put assortments of fruit on both plates, and hand him one. I get us some water and take my goods out of the oven to cool. Then I sit down and look at him again. He is deep in thought. He finally looks at me, but it is different from how he usually looks at me. It's serious. We typically are either flirting or joking around, never serious, so this is new.

"Are you ok?" I ask.

He stands up and then walks over to me. He leans down and kisses me senseless. When he backs away, it takes everything in me not to fall off the barstool. I jump into his arms, and we kiss deep and passionately. I can feel how hard he is already, and I am sure my panties are soaking wet. I wrap my legs around his waist, and then he pushes my back into the wall. Then he is taking off my night-shirt and sucking my nipples. I am grindin' into him something fierce, between this and my dreams last night, and lap dancing before he got here, I am about to combust. I unzip his pants and pull out his impressive dick, and he slides on protection as I suck his ear. Then he pushes my panties to the side, and he is sliding deep into my folds. I fill myself wrap around him as he slowly pushes into me. When he is all the way in, he sits snuggly inside and lets me get adjusted, all while he is licking and sucking on my neck. As I start to grind into him slowly, he is ready to turn it up. He begins to stroke me long and deep. I feel every inch of him with each stroke, and it blows my mind. I am screaming my pleasure and running my hands through his hair. Then he walks us to the couch and pulls out of me. He bends me over and pushes back into me in one stroke. I'm totally in my element, twerking and throwing my ass back at him as he smacks it. I love all he is doing, and I am screaming his name. I hear his groans as he keeps stroking me, and then I feel that wonderful feeling of an orgasm; it starts at my head then goes to my core, and then spreads to my pussy. I am on fire, and I am about to combust.

"JACK!!!! I'm cumming!!" I scream over and over again.

I feel him pull me to him as his strokes become erratic, and he licks my ear and says, "Me too, Sweetheart."

With that, we collapse on the soft with me on his lap. When our breathing finally becomes regular, he kisses my forehead. I look up into those caramel pools and smile at him. He smiles back.

"You want to order some lunch on Door Dash? We can have round two eat and then round three." He whispers into my ear.

"Don't threaten me with a good time. I guess we need lunch and dinner. Cause I plan to sit on this dick multiple times."

With that, he pulls out his phone, and we order lunch and preorder dinner, and then we get started with round two, which is perfect because I am already on his lap, ready to ride.

Chapter 4: Jack

I'm sitting in medivotion, a version of Christian meditation. I am taking my deep breaths and trying to quiet my mind. The past nine months have been crazy busy, from my moms and her men to work at EzeJ, our private jet charter company I co-own with my best friend Ezekiel, to this friend with benefits thing I have going on Trina to trying to find a house. The truth is, at my age, I feel like it is time to make some changes. So here I am with all this stuff running through my mind.

I tell myself to take a deep breath in through the nose and out through the mouth. Eventually, I find that calm place as I release all my thoughts to God and ask Him to sit with me. Truth be told, I probably should be asking Him for direction on what to do next, but I don't think I am ready for the answer. As much as I am talking about change, I am sure that God will require something I am not quite prepared for. Anyway, God obliges me for the moment and allows me to experience the peace of His presence. As I am finishing medivotion, my phone vibrates. Looking at the screen, I see it's Eze, aka Ezekiel.

"What it do, Bruh!!" I answer the phone as I get off the floor and blow out my copal incense.

"Nothing much, just making sure you are headed this way. The new jet is set to land in about 45 minutes. Bruh, I'm so hyped right now."

"Man, me too. I can't wait to see this thing. We have been doing well, but this is about to take us to the next level for sure."

We just purchased our biggest private jet yet, a Boeing 737. Our current fleet holds a couple of small jets and a few luxury midsize jets, but this new jet will open us up to more corporate accounts. The Boeing 737 can fly more people and provide a more luxurious experience. That means the hard part starts once the jet gets here. Now we need to go after more prominent clients. Don't get me wrong, I started this process before buying the jet, and some of our current clients are looking forward to the option. There is just more work. I feel like I have been just working and working, well that is outside of my new *friend*.

"So, Jack, you on your way, or will I be opening this gift alone?"

"Get off my phone, and I can head out, Bruh!" I laugh.

"Bet, see you in a few."

"Peace."

We hang up, and I put on my clothes. For some reason, I only do meditation in my underwear. It's like I can't get comfortable unless I am almost naked. Maybe that speaks to me undressing my thoughts or some shit. I don't know. The idea of undressing brings me back to the thoughts of my *friend*, Trina. Trina and I have been kickin' it. Hanging out, baking, going for runs and playing board games. She is cool, and the sex is bomb. So, we are just having fun. Neither of us is looking for anything to come of this. We are *friends*. However, every now and then, we have a moment. You know one where if you go left, you took the situation to relationship, but if you go right, you stay where you are. We always go right. This thought makes me chuckle as I lock the door to my luxury apartment and get on the elevator to go to the garage.

I get into my Rubellite Red Metallic Mercedes G 550 SUV with black 20-inch AMG multispoke wheels. I sit on the red leather seats and take a deep breath. This SUV always makes me feel hella grateful. To be honest, it was my dream whip. I wasn't sure if I would ever get it, but after Eze and I busted our butts for the last seven years building a multi-million-dollar business, I figured it was time I go ahead a treat myself. God has been good to me for real.

I plug in my phone and let Jill Scott flow through my speakers, keeping my mood light as we prepare to take care of some business. Rolling up to our hanger at the private airstrip we co-own, I park in my spot and head into the administrative building. Racheal, our receptionist, greets me.

"Hey boss man, the delivery will be here at 10am. Do you want me to take your coat?" She states as she runs her hand down my arm. When I look into her eyes, she licks her lips and gives me a smirk. This girl has been trying to tempt me from day one, but Eze and I agreed I would never sleep with our employees. Yeah, just me and not him; Eze is a one-woman man, and Lyric got that on lock. But this girl right here always got me second-guessing our agreement. She is always showing off the goods and touching me. I turn towards her and lean in to say, "Is that all you want?"

"Well, no. I will take something else if you are finally offering." Her voice turned sultry.

I don't know why I am entertaining her. Let me stop lying; yes, I do. I am stressed. Some people drink or eat when they are stressed, not me. I fuck, that's it. It helps me clear my mind. I shake my head. Obviously, I need to have some more medivotion because I am truly tripping.

I tell Racheal, "Naw, not today." As I give her a wink and then hand her my coat. When I look up, Eze is standing there shaking his head. I just chuckle and roll up my sleeves.

"We ready, Bruh?"

"We? Are you?"

"Yeah, man, let's do this. EzeJ is about to make new waves." We clap hands and head to the landing strip.

I would be lying if I said I didn't almost shed a tear. Watching this bird land and seeing it turn to the side and hold our logo on the tail was surreal. This is a dream come true for us both. As the door and the stairs let out, Racheal and the rest of our team, which includes administration, sales, marketing, and pilots, come out all with glasses in hand. Racheal passes Eze, me, and the pilot who flew in the new bird a glass of champagne, and we toast to new beginnings. Everyone cheers. We do our due diligence, check out everything, and make sure things look nice and as we ordered. Then we do the thing we have been dying to do since we found her, go strap up in the cockpit and take this beauty for a fly. She flies nicer than nice.

"Man, I can't believe this is us!" I hit Eze in the shoulder.

"Right!! This is life."

"I'm happy we did this. You know, bought her and everything."

"Yeah, but you've been stressing out for the past few months. Look, I know that this means more time for us building the company, but we are truly on the cusp of taking our business where we want, and then we can just let it coast."

"I know. I don't know what's been up with me." The truth is, I don't know why I have been this stressed. As I said, we have been working hard for the last few years, so nothing new on that end. Being two black men in the charter plane business ain't easy, but we are doing it. Something else is making me anxious, but I don't know what.

"Dude, you hear me?"

"What you say?"

He starts laughing at me. "I guess that's my answer. I was saying, what if we take this new plane and we go on vacation. We haven't had a good vacation since we started."

"That's a great idea. We can take her out in the open sky, and then we can have a vacation before we bust this grind."

"Bet. You know I must bring Lyric, and she will want to bring the girls. You good with that, or do I need to say this is a boys-only trip and take a hit." We both chuckle at that because if we said we were taking a full-fledge vacation without his wife, she would trip. Don't get me wrong, we go to Manpower retreats just like their Poweress retreats, but that ain't the same as a vacation.

"It's cool. Let's bring the whole gang. We can invite Vic too."

"Yeah, we haven't seen him in a grip."

"Ok, it's set. I contact Vic, and you talk to the women. Then we can do this. When do you want to go?"

"How about next week?"

"Bet." We say in unison as Eze lands the plane and all our employees cheer.

****

I'm sitting on my couch drinking a glass of Richard Hennessy and looking at the city skyline. Houston's skyline has its moments and being that one of my living room windows is all glass, and that glass extends to my bedroom, I get to catch a glimpse of that skyline every day.

Today was a great day; after we landed the plane, it was back to work, filling out papers, setting up meetings, the usual. As usual, I didn't get home until 8pm. So, after my shower, I just decided to sit. I really need to figure myself out. This weight

I am carrying, it's bugging me. I lean my head back against my sofa and just breathe, allowing the smooth jazz playing from the in-home system to fill my space. Then my phone vibrates. It's a note from the desk saying I have a visitor. Knowing it's probably my moms, I send the message to let her through. The knock comes 5 minutes later. I walk to the door in my basketball shorts and my house shoes. When I open the door, it's not moms at all.

Trina is one bad woman, from her soft silky golden almond skin to her curvy thighs and legs to her ample behind that is not too big but perfect for twerking and throwing it back to her soft yet firm mid-section due to her boot camp loving ass to her round breasts that are just enough to spill out my hand and fill up my mouth to her heart-shaped lips and almond-shaped eyes that are always covered in her lash extension, but not those porn ones the ones that make her lashes look like maybe they are hers to her waist-length natural hair she keeps blown out and flat ironed. Yeah, I have checked her out on many occasions, just as she does me. As a matter of fact, I am checking out the sway of her hips as she walks into my spot right now.

"Jack, did you hear me?"

I look up and see she is looking at me, concerned.

"Sorry, no, Sweetheart. What you say?"

"Jack, are you ok? I came over to help you turn up, but you look like someone stole yo bike." She smirks at me.

"Funny, says the woman who smells like a trash disposal," I smirk back.

"Oh, so you can smile. For your info, I came straight from the gym. I bought dinner. You said today we would be poppin' bottles to celebrate that big bird."

"Yeah." I look down at my shoes.

Trina looks at me. "What's up? Do you want me to leave?"

"It's not that, I just got a lot on my mind. I keep trying to clear it, but it's not working."

"You know I can help with that." She says, all sultry and rubbing her ass on me.

"Take your stinky butt on. Go take a shower. I'll warm up the food and then beat you in this game of Mortal Kombat."

"Boy, Bye, ain't no way you about to beat me. Let me catch this shower, and your ass is mine." She laughs as she walks out of the room and into the master bathroom since I only have one bedroom with a 1.5 bath.

To be honest, I didn't mind Trina in my space. Usually, I hated a girl in my space. Women tend to be all in your business looking for details that mean nothing to you but everything to them. Trina wasn't like that. She went with the flow and respected your space, just like she didn't press me just now.

I go into the kitchen and see what Trina brought for dinner. She is so bomb. She bought my favorite, Reggae Hut. I love the oxtails and peas and rice. Oh, and she got the coco bread. I start warming things up, which are mouthwatering from the start. I look in her other bags. There is Stella Rosa Moscato and Hennessy Black, maple syrup, and soda. Oh, she is going to mix my favorite drink, that Black Maple. The last bag has a small cake that says, "When I get to ride in the bird?" I burst out laughing.

I hear "Celebrate Good Times Come On", playing through my speakers just as the microwave beeps. This girl cracks me up every time. She comes around the corner in one of those girly onesies with ears, the start of the holiday kind of pajamas. I fall out laughing.

"Dude, what kind of party is dis?" I laugh.

"The lighten your mood and have you ready to cele-chill kind." She is shaking her little tail on the onesie to the music.

"Cele-chill?"

"Yeah, you know, like celebrate and chill." I chuckle at her antics. "I knew you were either turnt up, or you were chilled out. So, I came ready for both. Plus, you sounded like you needed to cheer up when we talked earlier." She shakes her tail again and rubs it against me. "How am I doing?"

"Perfect." I bring her in for a hug. She always seems to know how to lighten up my day. I reach around her and see she is holding a present bag. "What's this?"

"Your gift. Open it!!"

When I open it, it is a pair of AirPod pros engraved to say That Bird, Though. I burst out laughing. Then at the bottom of the bag is a container; I moan out loud.

"OH, and it's warm too. How did you?" I open the lid, and it's my favorite chocolate chip red velvet macaroons. During one of our baking moments, we started making different variations, and this one is the one for me. I take a bite and groan into its goodness. She put some rum in my macaroon. I hug her and give her kisses all over her face.

"If all else failed, I knew you would love the macaroons," She laughs as she heads to the kitchen to check on the food.

"Thank you, Tri. These are bomb, and you know I was still in my feelings about my AirPods. So good lookin out." Last month we were at the gym about to race in the pool, and since I wasn't trying to get beat, I rushed to jump in, forgetting my AirPods were in my shorts. It had me mad as hell when I lost, and my Airpods didn't work.

She smiled over at me as she ate one of the oxtails. We sat at the bar and enjoyed each other's company. We talked about our day, and I showed her pics of the new plane. We decided against video games because we both were tired after eating, that "'it is" ain't no joke. We agreed on Netflix instead. We ended up rewatching the Bridgertons. My guilty pleasure, no one knew but her. No one knows how chill we have gotten. They know we shared a night but not that we have been hanging out as friends. It's kind of nice that way, like having a friend that none of your other friends can interfere with.

We are watching Season 1 Episode 3, and Trina is lying on top of me. I adjust her on my chest, and she looks up.

"You good?"

"Better than good. Thanks for this. I was trippin' earlier."

"No worries. I got you." She kisses my hand and then lays back down.

We fall asleep, letting Bridgerton watch us.

Chapter 5: Jack

"Moms, where you at?"

"In the back, taping up these boxes."

As I walk to the back, I hear her screen door in the kitchen open.

"You expecting someone?"

"Trina has the leotards for the girls."

I make it into the room with my moms. I give her a kiss on the cheek and then stack some boxes and pick them up.

"Jackson, I am so excited about this new studio. I don't know what to do. The teachers are great, and students have already signed up."

"Moms, it's your dream to own yo own spot. I'm proud of you." I kiss her forehead. Trina walks in the room looking good enough to eat, wearing tight-as-skin yoga pants and a crop top. I can see her belly ring with every step she takes. It's been a hot minute since we actually did anything sexual, but right now, I want to umm.

"Ms. Kathy, you ready to turn this studio out!!"

"Hey, Baby, you know I am. We bout to show this youngin's how to make it werk." My moms starts twerking. I use the boxes and cover my eyes.

"Moms, seriously?"

"Boy, how you think you got here?" She laughs. I shake my head.

"See, that is why you need to slow down on these dudes. Out here being a panther."

"Boy, you right. I may stop having boyfriends but a boy toy…."

"Moms, stop." She is laughing her butt off. I am just standing there deadpanning her.

"Fine, Jackson. Calm down. I was thinking the same thing." She walks over and smiles at me, patting me on the shoulder. After a few minutes, Trina closes a box and then walks over and asks, "Hey Jack. You need help?"

"Hey Tri, yeah, grab that box by the door. Moms, is this it?"

"And that box that Trina put in my kitchen." You could hear all her irritation when she said that.

"Gurl, you bout to get your visitation privileges revoked, putting stuff other than food in her kitchen." Trina hits me in the arm.

"Shut up! But you right, go get that box." We both started laughing as we went toward the kitchen. We switched who was carrying what and headed to my SUV. Once we got everything inside, I backed Trina against the boxes before closing the trunk.

"What are you doing," she said, looking around.

"How you thought you were coming over here smelling like Creed Aventus for Her and having on no panties, and I can't touch?"

"I do have on panties, thank you." She smirks at me as I push my body flush against her.

"Trina, I keep telling you a v string ain't no panties."

"Whatever." We stare at each other for a little bit. The air between us thickens.

"Come by after y'all get done at the studio?" I say, nuzzling her neck.

"I'm sorry I can't; I'm going out with Erica to search for men." I lean back, and she is smiling.

"So, you gone go looking for some dick, when I am offering you clean, can't walk tomorrow, knock you out, put a smile on your face dick, right here? That's what you doing?"

"As much as you are tempting, *friend*, I need to go help my girl find someone."

"And you?"

"Why you asking?"

"Curious."

"Jealous?"

"Naw," I look down, then back up, "just checking out your plans." Gratefully moms takes that moment to call out."

"Yall got it all packed out here?"

"Yes, Ma'am," we say in unison.

"Good, let's get this show on the road. Jack, I'm riding with you. One of the teachers is bringing me home later."

"Alright." My moms starts locking up. I look at Tri, and she has this weird look on her face. "Why are you looking at me like that?"

"Nothing," she states softly and shakes her head. "I'll follow y'all there." With that, she walks away.

****

"Y'all did your thing with this grand opening."

"That was my Trina. She is really good at planning. She had all the details worked out for me. I let her do her thing."

"She did that then." I searched the crowd with my eyes, but I didn't see Trina. The truth is I haven't seen her since we unloaded the SUV. It is almost like she is avoiding me. Then I see her talking to some little girl's dad. I guess that's who he is. She is smiling all in his face, and he is smiling down at her like he wants to eat her. For some reason, this really bothers me. I mean, I have seen her flirt before. Shoot, we have even been each other's wingman. So why is this bugging me, seriously? I am one step away from going over there and busting this up because ole' dude is not her type anyway. When I move to go over there, my moms says, "Y'all ain't slick, you know?"

I look at her with my eyebrows bunched. "What are you talking about?"

"Come on here, Jackson. I raised you. I know when you are up to something." She looks into my eyes and then at Trina.

"Moms, you off base with this one."

"Really, so you weren't just about to go over there and interrupt the flirting they doing?"

"What? No, I was going to go to help Mama Lynda pass out the cake."

"Riiight," Moms says, shaking her head and patting my shoulder. "Well, I am just gone say this. Whatever yall got going on needs to be tightened up. Ain't no need in having feelings if you not gone do nothing about it. Plus, she is a good catch, if she will have you."

"Enough, Moms, we are friends, that's it." I walk off and help Mama Lynda pass out the cake. Mama Lynda is a second mom to me. She is Ezekiel's mom. To be honest, we kind of look out for each other's moms because they can definitely get into their own sort of trouble since they can't seem to stay out of grown folks' business.

"Mama L, that's the last one," I say as I clean off the table and throw away the trash.

"Thank you, Darling. You feeling, ok? You look a little tired. You and Eze work too hard sometimes. Before you give me the spiel, I know it takes time and hard work to build a company. I just don't want you to look up, and life has passed you by. You are too good of a man for that." She says as she pats my cheek.

"I'm alright, don't worry about me."

"You know, you lying to an ole' woman. That just ain't right." She laughs and picks up some more trash, and throws it away.

"Alright, how about I say, just pray for me, and eventually I will be alright."

She turns around and looks me in the eyes with one of her sweet smiles. She hugs me and says, "Always am Darlin. Let me know if you need anything else. Tell your Mom I will see her later." She releases me and turns to pick up her purse. I turn and see that Trina is packing up the registration stuff, and another dude is all in her face, making her smile and laugh. She turns and catches me staring, and there is that weird look again. I turn to Mama L, and she is staring dead at me, and she says, "Darlin, I do my best to stay out of y'all's love lives but be careful with that one. She will either give you the world or tear you apart. Make sure you know what you are doing."

With that, she pats my chest and walks on around me. I decide to walk her out since she is the only one leaving, and she doesn't say anything else about it. I kiss her cheek, and off she goes. As I walk back into the studio, I start to think about what she said. I get it. Trina is the kind of woman who will love you hard and give you the world, but that makes her vulnerable, so she does what I do have no strings attached kind of relationships. Then the people you are with really don't know you outside of what you can do in the bedroom.

Maybe that's my problem. Since I have been kickin it with Trina, I haven't really been looking for anyone else. I think it is time to fix that. I hit up my boy Vic and see if he wants to hit a club or two with me tonight. Eze and I used to do it, but he is married, so that's out the question. As I reach my moms to tell her bye, I get Vic's message in the affirmative. Oh yeah, tonight should be fun. We agree to meet at the club.

Chapter 6: Trina

"Erica, you sure about this? I mean, I like the strip club as much as anyone else, but it's not really your scene. I thought you wanted to hit up a lounge or something?"

"Well, Tri, that hasn't been working. Maybe it is time to change the harvest field."

"The fruit in here may not be that good, though. The strip club is where you pick and lick, but don't bite and digest, you understand?"

"Trina, I thought you would be down with this. I just want to try something different that's it. Can you please just go with my flow?" She says, tired of me with my antics.

"Alright, let's do this." We take a few shots before we catch the Uber to Club Duo. Club Duo is a co-ed strip club and club. Level 1 is the club, where all the regular dancing occurs, and the main bar and DJ are located. On Level 2, there is the gentleman's club with the female strippers, and Level 3 is the ladies club with the male strippers. Each level has private rooms, so if you want to get a little more intimate with your partner or a stripper, you can. Obviously, I have been there before. If I am honest, I used to go all of the time. I just haven't really been feeling the scene as of late. But tonight is about my girl letting down her hair and finding a man at least for a minute.

I look at Erica across the back seat from me. She is gorgeous, but she is also needy and insecure. A man picks up on both things right away and either uses them or leaves the woman alone. I, on the other, have bucket loads of confidence and self-love, so I am always getting asked out like I got three numbers at the studio earlier. They were fine too, but I am not quite ready to date a man with kids, so that's out. I guess I am prowling tonight, too, especially since Jack was being all weird today. But we are not thinking about that. As we pull up to the club, I check my lipstick and makeup, and Erica and I get out of the car. I smooth out my Herve Leger Bandage knit mini dress. I must admit this dress fits me like a second skin. It shows off my thickness just right, including my little midsection. I love the gym, but I love to bake too, so I am forever a size 12-14, and to be honest, I love it. It's me. My red bottoms hit the concrete like they are alerting all the men to our arrival. With my hair pulled in a high ponytail, I look delicious, and as we enter the club, the men's eyes tell me just how much.

We walk up to the bar and get two sunsets on the beach. Yep, it is a tequila kind of night.

"Gurl, this place is bomb. Why you never bought me here. I love how low the lights are and the dark purple and gray accents they have going on. This DJ is nice too."

"You always tell me no. Ole' Bougie one." I shout.

"Shut up!!" she hits me playfully. "My bad, my boughetto friend." We both start laughing.

They start playing one of my jams, "Wet the bed," and we both run to the dance floor, gyrating and singing along. This guy scoots up behind me, and I bend over a little bit and have a good time dancing with him. I had to slow down, though, because he couldn't keep up. Most men can't. I look up and see that Erica got a friend too. We dance with the same dudes for about five songs, then the dude tries to nibble on my neck. Now, I know I have been grinding on him, but that disgusted me for some reason. As soon as the song ends, I tell Erica I am going to the bathroom, and she decides to come with me.

"Alright, Boo, I see you out there. I didn't know you knew how to dance like that."

"Only at home. But I am changing it up. What you think?"

"You know I am good, but don't lose yourself looking for a dude. The right one will come along. And love you for you."

"Says the girl with a new man every three months." The lady washing her hands next to me laughs. I give her a bad side-eye. She shuts up quickly and leaves in a hurry. I don't know why she thought she was a part of this conversation, anyway.

"True, just saying. Anyway, you ready to find some more men."

"Absolutely," we say in unison and clap hands.

We head back to the bar and decide to get another round and then head to Level 3. On Level 3, the men look delicious enough to eat. Like take your finger, and the chocolate will melt your yoni kind of hot. We sit down and watch the dancer do a magic-mike-themed performance. He is doing the doggone thing. We decided to move closer to the stage and threw some money on it because the performance was going so good. The next dancer is even sexier, and he is rolling his body just how you would want it. I think Erica is about to pass out when he comes off the stage and starts dancing on her.

"Gurl, don't be shame to grab all that chocolate," I yell over the music. "Yaasss!! Fuck her up!" My gurl is a puddle in this dancer's hands. I am making it rain all over him as he grinds into her.

Then I feel someone press into me and say in a deep smooth voice that gets me every time, "So throwing ones is your thing?"

That familiar scent of Aventus Cologne by Creed with his own special undertones has me gone before he even puts his hands on me. Then he grabs my waist and pulls me flat against him. It's aggressive and possessive, and I like it. He starts to dance with me as the song's bass speeds up. We are grinding in sync, my hands are in his hair, and his tongue is sliding along my ear and occasionally dips inside. He is so hard, and it feels so good. Then he says, "Bathroom now."

He lets me go abruptly, and he walks off. I turn and see that Erica is still in a daze, and the dancer has started round two. So, I slip away. The moment I walk in and lock the one-stall bathroom, we are kissing, and he picks me up, puts me on the counter, and tears my panties off. The look in his eyes is possessive and primal, and it makes me moan. He pulls his pants down and then plunges into me in one stroke. The sex is fast and reckless, not caring who hears us and oh so satisfying as we cum together.

When our breathing comes down, he kisses my forehead, my ear, and then my lips.

"Trina, you look damn good tonight." His voice is thick and sexy. He steps back and is adjusting his clothes and looking at me.

I close my legs and hop down to get some paper towels to clean up with, "Thank you, Jackson." I smirk at him through the mirror. He smirks back.

"Sorry I couldn't keep my hands to myself."

I turn and hug him close. "Never apologize for that. That was amazing."

He hugs me tight. "I'm about to head out. You need a ride, or you good?"

"Let me check with Erica. We came together."

"I thought that was her. She is faded."

I laugh as we walk out of the restroom. My girl is still sitting in her seat, but now she is going through her phone. Jack goes to the bar, so it is not obvious to my friend what just happened. Our other friends don't know about us hanging out, and I kind of like it that way. With Jackson, I can be my true self and get some good D all simultaneously. Other people complicate that since we are all friends. I think it's just an unspoken thing we have going on, not to tell them.

"Hey, Boo, how you feel getting yourself rubbed and grinded on?" I say as I twerk down but stop because the sweet soreness between my legs starts reminding me of what I just did.

"That was everything!!" We laugh. "I think I am ready to head out, though. I am getting tired."

"Well, it is 3am, so that's understandable."

"Alright, let me get us an uber."

"Naw, I ran into Jack over there. He said he would take us home." She looks behind her, and he waves at her. She stands, "Gurl, that man is finer than fine. Let's go!"

"That he is" is my reply as we walk toward him.

****

We dropped off Erica first, and now we are at my loft. Jack walks me to my door, and then when I come in and leave it open for him, he doesn't come in.

"Hey Jack, you coming in?"

He looks me in my eyes, and I can tell he wants to ask me something, but he is deciding if he really wants to know or not. Something is changing between us. Things seem to be intensifying, and usually, this is when I would leave, but with Jack, I just want to smooth out his thoughts and fears. He shakes his head and then comes in and closes and locks the door.

I go to my room to shower, and Jack goes to the kitchen probably to get a drink. The next thing I know, the shower door is opening, and Jack is getting inside. He looks at me so intensely I feel like I am melting under his gaze. He takes my towel and begins to bathe me, slow and steady. It's so erotic and intimate. We have never done this before, showered together. It is one of those things we both think is for couples, but here we are. When he is finished cleaning me thoroughly, he kisses me just as thoroughly. Then I wash him with the same detail and gentleness he showed me. We get out and dry off and lotion up, and then we get into bed and cuddle without any clothes.

"Goodnight, beautiful."

"Goodnight, Jackson. "

He kisses my ear and pulls me close. This feels amazing is the last thought I have as I doze off.

Chapter 7: Trina

The next morning, I wake up nestled against Jackson's firm chest and inhale his natural scent. This is not the first time we shared a bed, but it is the first time that we have cuddled. We did some serious spooning last night, and now my head is on his chest, and my leg is thrown over his. One of his arms is wrapped around my body with his hand close to my behind, and his other hand is on my arm that is around his chest. It is almost like I wanted to be on him, and he wanted to keep me there. The truth is I had the best sleep than I have had in months while being wrapped in his arms. If I am being honest, I sleep well every time we share a bed. It is like his mere presence soothes a part of me that no one can touch. What we are doing now feels so natural, so right, like home.

That thought has me wanting to get up. It scares me, no lie. I try to move slowly so I don't wake him; he is not a morning person learned that too many times. But as soon as I move, his hold on me tightens.

"Tri, stay there." His voice is deep and groggy since I woke him up.

"Jack, I need to pee," I say softly.

He groans in response but releases me. I go to the bathroom. When I come out, he is back sleeping. I grab my laptop and tiptoe out of the room. I sit at the bar and scroll through my emails, trying to stop the thought that began in the bed about Jackson feeling like home. As I scroll, I see an email from the Poweress Committee. I open it, and it says,

Hey Poweress,

It feels like some of us could use a nice mini-retreat to relax and refocus and be honest with ourselves. It is hard to constantly walk true to who you are if you are not really being honest with yourself. This mini-retreat will focus on being honest with yourself and give you the tools needed to do that. We know it is short notice, but the retreat is next week, and we only have 10 slots available. Please send us an email if you are interested, and we will get you on the road to finding the Power of Truth.

Speak with you soon,

Your Poweress Committee.

I read the email again. Truth is, I need this. There is no lying to myself about that. I am actually sitting here right now because I am trying to not be honest with myself. So, I responded to the email and got an email back with the cost and location. The mini-retreat is in Key West, Florida, so that is good. I look at the price, it is a little out of my budget, but I know I will be better when I leave the retreat than when I get there. So, I put my card info in the slot on the website officially booking the retreat and then booked my flight. I also draft an email to my boss asking for the time off. The retreat is only three days which is good, but I request a week. As I finish up, Jack kisses my ear, comes around to the kitchen, and pours himself some juice.

"What you workin' on?"

"Nothing much." He is looking at me and pouring me a glass of juice which he knew I would ask for. He turns on the coffee machine, which is usually the first thing I do. I guess that is proof that my thought process in bed has me all messed up.

"So, we bout to do this Power marathon or what? I still can't believe you haven't seen it." He hands me the juice and starts pulling stuff out for omelets.

"I know, I was busy. Can you add bacon to my omelet this time? I like veggies, but dang." I laugh at him.

He smacks his teeth and looks over his shoulder, "Whatever, you like my omelets, but I will honor the request." He starts cutting up the veggies. He is actually a great cook. One of his secret loves that he doesn't tell his ladies. He always says a woman expects you to do all the cooking once she finds out you got skills. He ain't lying. I know I show do. But he cooks, and I bake; it's a tradeoff.

"Hey, what were you doing on level 3 last night? Is there something you need to tell me?" I say with my chin in my hands and watching his back, and arm muscles flex as he makes our food. He has on some basketball shorts he left here last time.

"Man, I was on Level 2 with Vic, but I got up to go to the restroom and thought I saw you walk by. So I went to check it out, and sure enough, you were there throwing out ones." He starts making it rain invisible money.

I throw some napkins at him. "Shut up!! I was hyping Erica up."

"I can't believe your gurl was there. That don't even look like her spot."

"I know, but she wants to try something different." I walk over and start running my hands through his curly hair. I love his hair. It is soft and curls around your fingers. You just want to get lost in it time and time again. He leans into my hands and moans softly. He likes head massages on both heads. Lol.

"Man, she can't be desperate if she wants someone to holla at her."

"I know dis, but she thinks you Fine, though."

He gives me the death stare. "Man, get out of here with that." He shakes my hands out of his hair.

"When we sit to watch the show, you want me to give you some braids? I know you asked last week, but work had me busy."

"Yeah, let's do it."

We eat and then get situated with him between my legs, with me on the couch and him on the floor. As he found the show, I got the hair products organized. When I was in college, I made lots of spare money doing braids for people. I got a lot of play from boys doing their hair too. Jack and I were hanging out one day, and I started messing around in his hair, and he liked it. Now I tended to do it for him from time to time.

We were watching one episode. I promise it was almost porn. It got me all wet and everything. At that point, Jack was sitting on the couch, and my feet were in his lap. He started making small circles like he was thinking the same thing that I was. One of the beautiful parts of friends with benefits is you can take the benefits at any moment, and that moment was no different. Because now, he is hitting it from the back off the edge of the sofa, and I am screaming his name. Then there is a knock at the door.

"Don't stop. Please don't stop. I'm right there." He reaches around and squeezes my clit gently, making me cum just as the knock comes again with the last voice I expect to hear.

"Baby Girl, open the door. I have to pee." I push him back just as he starts laughing.

"Coming, Mom, give me one second."

He helps me spray, I fix my clothes, and then he goes and hides in the back.

I open the door to see my mom and my dad. Really right now, people, is what I groan on the inside.

"Hey yall, what you doing here?" I say as my mom kisses my cheek and heads to the bathroom. My dad hugs me, and I make sure to turn to the side.

"Well, I was in Dallas on business, so I thought why not come down and see you. We were hoping you may have some time for your parents."

"Oh, Daddy," I say as my mom reenters.

"Hey Baby, we were going to ask you to lunch, but" she looks at the bar and sees the two plates we had not cleaned. Then she looks at the coffee table and sees the two cups of coffee. Oh hell, this is about to be some mess. "It looks like you already ate, and you have company in here somewhere." She yells to make sure said company hears her.

"Well, let's meet this young man. If he deserves to be here eating and lounging with you all day, he should be good enough for us to meet." My dad states matter of fact. He is so going into lawyer mode. It is one of the reasons why I never bought a man home after the first time. In high school in Atlanta, I brought home my first real boyfriend. My dad interrogated him so badly, it was like he was on trial, and that was it. We didn't stand a chance. My father would pop up on our dates, and my mom would call the whole time. It drove my boyfriend and me crazy. Eventually, he moved on and said my people brought too much baggage. I was hurt, but I understood. My parents kept me on close watch. So yeah, as soon as I made it to U of H, I wilded out. Parties, one-night stands, all that. Then I met my girls, and they made me calm down a little because I still partied and had one-night stands, just not as often. They thought I was wild and didn't care about my work, but no one messed with that. I had goals to become somebody. The problem was and still is, I don't know what that somebody is, though. Plus, my parents were not having me drop out. So, I got an MBA at their request, but I have done nothing with it.

They both are staring at me like they expect me to get my guest, but that we are not doing.

"Well, who said it was a guy or that the company is still here."

"Oh, honey, is that why you haven't brought anyone home. You need to come out to us?" My mom uses her freshly manicured hand and strokes my hair.

"Baby girl, we can manage that too."

My parents, well, my family is wealthy. Most people don't know that because once they know, it turns our friendship into being about money. But that is the reason I have been able to go from job to job and buy all the name brands I want. I have a trust. I haven't used it all, but shop therapy is definitely my thing.

"You guys stop," I say, removing my mom's hand as I speak. "I am not in the closet, and there is nothing to manage."

"Oh, praise God because I was not trying to deal with all of that today." My father states. Already ready to call in favors to keep the family name intact. This is why they meet no one, not even my friends, and they don't see me. I can only take so much.

As if Jackson can hear me drowning, he appears from the back wearing his jeans and tailored business shirt from last night and a blazer that I may or may not have taken from his house because it was a bomb, and I wanted to make it mine. He looks sexy as all get out like he just got back from making multi-billion dollar lunch deals. He pulled his braids back and made a man bun to finish off the look. I accidentally lick my lips cause Damn.

"Hey Baby, sorry about that. You know I have been trying to close this deal all week." He kisses my cheek and then turns those pools of caramel on my mother, and I swear she melts too.

"Ms. Davenport, it is truly a pleasure to meet you. I can see where Tri gets her beauty from." My mom giggled like a schoolgirl. Jackson is laying it on thick, and I am so grateful he is. The only thing he knows about my family is that they are stuck up, and my father is a lawyer.

He extends his hand to my dad, "Mr. Davenport, a pleasure to make your acquaintance."

"And you are?" Here we go.

"Jackson Anthony co-owner of EzeJ charter planes and boyfriend to your lovely daughter Katrina." With that, he puts his hand low on my back and kisses my forehead. Then the men shake hands. My father is sizing him up, but Jack stands his ground. I am assuming this is what he looks like in the board room because the confidence and power coming off of him are palpable and sexy as hell.

"So, how long have you and my daughter been a thing?"

Jack looks into my eyes and then says, "We started as friends and have recently, over the last month, become more than that." What the world is he saying?

"Well, young man, I have heard of your business. It is one of the best. My firm has been looking to get in contact with you and start a partnership."

Jack releases me and pulls his business card out of his pocket, "Have your people call us. When you call, tell them I sent you. You will get in easily after that."

"Well, thank you. Do you live around here?" Really! Where are all of the questions?

"Not too far. I am closer to the medical center."

"House?"

"Actually, I am in the market now. It is definitely time to make that move." When Jack says this, I hear my mom take a deep breath, and then she says, "Why is that? Jackson, is it?"

"Yes, ma'am, it is Jackson. I think it is time for me to settle down and get ready for the next step in life." He looks down into my eyes and winks. What the hell is he doing? I try to say this with my eyes as my mother is clenching her pearls with joy. However, my father is back in interrogation mode, "Are you saying you would like to cohabitate with my daughter. I did no..." Jack cuts him off.

"Oh no, sir. I respect Tri too much for that. I am looking to make things more official than that." He turns and smirks at me. My father looks pleased, while I am about to have a fit. I need to stop this.

"Well, there you go." I start.

"Jackson, we were about to go for a late lunch. Would you care to join us?" My mother offers. I never agreed to this lunch. Another reason I don't go see them. They like to run everything like I am not in my 30s.

"I would love to, but duty calls. I was actually about to leave." He shakes their hands and is all smiles, and then he turns to me, "Baby, can you walk me out?" I nod my head yes. I am so done with him.

On the one hand, I appreciate the help, but on the other hand, he just made a mess for me to clean up. When we get outside to his SUV, I let him know it too.

"Jack, what the world!! You couldn't stop at saying you are my man. You had to insinuate that we are at the point of marriage?" I say, hitting him in the shoulder.

He chuckles. "Hey, that seemed to be the only way to keep from getting more questions. You're welcome."

"I didn't thank you for that."

"You should be because your parents are intense. The only thing that saved me was my company and my "high" interest in marrying you."

"Whatever," I say, pouting.

He pulls me into his body and kisses my ear. "Sorry, I have to go. Things were getting good."

I look up into his eyes, and there is that look again. The one that says I want you for more than what I am telling you. The look that says be mine. I shake off my thoughts and look at the floor, "I understand. Well, holla at me later," I say as I move to walk away. He catches me by the wrist, then pulls me to the SUV placing my back against the car, he kisses me like he really kisses me. One of those toe-curling I could fall in love and cum just from a kiss kisses. What is going on here? He steps back and smiles at me. He gets in the SUV and drives off.

I walk back to my loft, confused as all get out.

Chapter 8: Jack

I am in Eze's office nursing a glass of Remy Martin after our long work week. We are looking out at the planes in the hanger. It was a good week. We scheduled lots of meetings and had lots of meetings. Business is going well, and the new bird is making us money already. We had to cancel our vacation idea after people started booking the plane from the moment it became listed. Trina's father firm, Davenport & Davenport, is now one of the companies we have under contract. The last week was busy, and I haven't really talked to Trina. She is at the Poweress mini-retreat, and I miss her. It is crazy.

"Bruh, what's on your mind?" Eze says.

"How do you go from friends to more?"

"What do you mean?"

"Don't you dare laugh." He is already laughing, and I haven't said anything yet. "I think I have feelings for Trina." Full-blown laugh now. "Man, forget you." I flip him off.

"I'm sorry……. Ok." He takes a deep breath and then looks at me. "What kind of feelings?"

"I'm falling for her, slowly but surely. I was trying to stop it, but the more we hang out and share, the more I find out she is amazing." I look out at the hanger.

I feel him staring at me. He doesn't say anything for a while. The truth is my last real relationship was in college. I thought this girl would be my wife until I found her in bed with my roommate. Since then, I have just been chilling, not looking for more, just coasting, but something is going on between me and Tri that has me questioning things. For instance, I have never showered with a woman, but I showered with her. Bathed her, even. I truly enjoyed sleeping in her bed holding her. It felt like home like I was going to be ok.

Eze is watching me closely. "Do you love her?"

"I think I have love for her."

"You know what I mean."

"I don't know."

"Well, when you figure that part out, you will know what to do next. Love has a way of taking you on its journey. You don't control it. You just go along for the ride. Once you know the hard part is done."

With that, we pour another round and enjoy the smooth liquid.

Chapter 9: Trina

Walking into my hotel room, I am wrapped in the scent of warm vanilla. It makes me want to sit and grab a nice blanket and cuddle up. Of course, I can't, though. In true Poweress committee fashion, there is already an itinerary on my desk with a beautiful black leather clutch with intricate designs of lilies embossed into the leather. On the clutch's bottom right is the words Poweress embossed in silver with the gold butterflies hanging off the last 's'.

I look at the itinerary, and it states:

Welcome, Poweress,

This mini-retreat is meant to help you relax, find your honesty, and give you the courage to speak your honest truths to yourself. We hope that after this, you will have the desire to actually walk in the truth that you speak. Below you will find tonight's festivities.

Day 1

7p-9p: Dinner in the Marvel Room

9p-11p: Sister Circle and prep for tomorrow in the Relaxation Room

11p: Go back to rooms for sleep.

P.S. We dropped a little gift in your bag for today. Please get it before you come.

I always love the gifts at these things. I have been to a couple of these mini-retreats and one big retreat over the years. I always leave feeling like I am ready for what is next in my life. Hopefully, this time is no different.

I open the clutch and find the inside has a deep purple velvet lining. It feels soft and smooth to the touch. I find that there are three gifts wrapped in white tissue paper. I take out the one marked Day 1. When I open it, I see a small ring that says courage, written in cursive. The ring is two-toned, gold and silver encasing diamonds that write out the word courage. The ring is perfect for my pointing finger, so I decide to put it on. Then I read the note.

Poweress,

This ring is to remind you that courage is inside of you. You can be honest with yourself and walk in the truth. You already have what you need on the inside. The Power of

Truth is one that cannot be denied. So don't take away that power that keeps pushing you and leads you to purpose, love, and destiny because you are lying to yourself. Poweress, it is time to walk in truth. God is ready to reveal things to you, have the courage to take heed.

Peace, Love, & Courage,

Poweress Committee

This letter is so true and speaks to exactly why I am here. I need to figure out what is happening in and around me; well, I need time to sit and be honest with myself about what is going on in and around me. I kiss my new ring and look at the time. It is 7:05. I am late for dinner. So, I put my room key in the back pocket of my high-waisted wide-leg jeans and pick up my phone, and I am on my way.

****

Walking into the Marvel Room for dinner, I am happy that I kept on my cropped black jacket over my graffiti cropped tank because it is cold in here. I find my name tag at a table in the back, just as they pass out the salads. I speak to everyone and take a drink of wine. There are 3 other ladies at my table, and we make small talk over dinner. I will be honest I was not feeling them. I like to turn up with others and deal with myself by myself, so this whole let's share what is wrong with me thing with them is not working. Anyway, I am nice though. After dinner, I see Tiff, a woman that Lyric met at her first retreat and that we met on the cruise.

"Hey hey, Hot thang!!" I greet her.

"Hey, Boo!! I'm so happy you are here. Some of these women ask too many questions. It's like, gurl, let me figure it out." She says as we hug.

"Right, I was just thinking the same thing. Where yo gurl at?"

"Rina had to work. What about yo peeps?"

"To be honest, I don't even know. I booked it and didn't share."

"Sometimes it be that way."

We are laughing and catching up as we go to the Relaxation Room for our Sister Circle.

Tiff looks my way before we part, "Let's hook up before we leave."

"Absolutely."

We give each other a pound and then find our assigned places.

When I sit, I am underly surprised. I did not tell any of my friends I was coming because, honestly, I needed to figure out some things without a watchful eye. There are many things about my life and me that they don't know. It's not like I'm hiding. It's just that I learned a long time ago people can't always be trusted with your truth. Shoot, sometimes you can't be trusted with your truth.

I sit down next to the person who is to be my partner. It looks like even though this is a Sister Circle, they are trying to give us the intimacy to share. So, you are only talking to one person. Since we are not supposed to know each other because things were picked randomly, there should be an air of confidentiality. However, we will see how this works out for me.

I sit in front of a person I could not mistake for anyone else if I tried. She is one of my besties.

"So, Boo, you stocking me?" I say as I sit. She looks up and bursts out laughing.

"Gurl, stop!!! What are you doing here?"

"I guess the same as you. Since you didn't share with the group, I guess you were hiding away too."

"Gurl, sometimes you need to think without all the eyes."

"I feel that for reals. Look, Boo, we can get them to switch us."

She takes a moment and then says, "Naw Tri, I think this may serve us well. You know they usually know what they are doing when they pair people."

"You right, Liza. They usually pair people well. Ok, let's agree that whatever happens here stays between us."

"Absolutely." We shake hands to solidify our agreement and then hug.

"Good evening, Poweress'. My name is Christine. It is truly a pleasure to be here and assist you on your journey of truth with yourself. Before we get started, let me tell you how this will go. You are all getting a customized black leather journal matching the clutches you found in your room. The journals and the matching pens are being passed out to you now. These journals are what you are to use as you take this journey of truth. We will begin with going into mediation and medivotion. Medivotion is the extra step where meditation takes you into the presence of God so that you can hear from Him. There is no better place to find truth and be set free than in God's presence. With that being said, in a few minutes, I will have you grab both hands of the lady next to you, and when we begin breathing, you guys will do so on the same accord. The lady you are sitting with is your partner and support as you go through this journey. You can allow them to be as supportive or not as you need them to be. Tonight, the goal is to open you up and begin the process of being honest with you, but this retreat is about action. Therefore, tomorrow you will share at least some of your truth with your fellow Poweress. This way, you have said it with your mouth and fully have to accept it. After tonight's session of breathwork and holding space with the lady next to you, you will go to your room and find that a private yoni steam has been set up for you, and there you will use your journal to begin to write your truths. Are there any questions?" She waited for a pause. There were no questions.

The committee came back out with gold and silver scarfs and handed each of us one, and then they came back one more time and handed us each a lapis lazuli mala necklace. Then, Christine started again.

"Now you have scarfs and lapis lazuli mala necklaces that can be used however you want to use them during this time. All I ask is that both of them are on your person. Now we will begin. Please face the woman next to you and make eye contact. Look into each other's eyes and feel the walls between you begin to drop." She pauses.

I am looking into Liza's eyes, and for the first time, I see the true sadness that lays behind them. I see the hope and the loss. The strength and the weakness. I see her. I feel like she is looking into my soul as her brown eyes analyze my being. I feel the wall that protects my real person crumbling, and as much as I want to stop the process, I know this is precisely what I need. I also know this is the reason that we would work best together. If I have to get naked in front of someone, I needed it to be someone I know. I am grateful that God knew exactly what I needed even in my running.

Christine begins again, "Now grab each other's hands and allow the energy between you to connect." Again, a pause.

I feel the energy as soon as I grab her hands. It makes us move closer to each other. I can tell she felt it, too, as her expression became very curious.

"Now, please take some deep breaths with me, in through your nose and out through your mouth. Again." There is a pause. "Again. Now close your eyes and allow your breathing to sync with your partner's. Breathe together and continue to hold hands."

This is starting to feel really intense. I am opening up, and I feel my emotions coming to the forefront. It is like we are touching and agreeing to become honest with ourselves, holding each other up to do just that.

Christine continues, "Allow the presence of God to surround you. Feel His peace and insight and wisdom being imparted into you. Allow Him to be the third member of your group."

I feel God. I feel His strength, and I feel His arms wrapping around me. Then I hear Him say, "Tri stop running from the truth. Open up and receive it." With that, the tears begin to fall. I try to suck it up, but I can't. They are streaming down my face then I hear Liza say, "Oh God." It is of awe and pain. I hear her crying, which makes me cry more for my friend and me.

Christine leaves us in this space for I am not sure how long, and then she says, "Now go back to your synced breathing, taking in deep breaths in through your nose and out through your mouth. Do this seven times." After ample time she continues, "Now release each other's hands and feel yourself resting in the strength that the connection between your partner, God, and you has created. Now is the time to use the scarf and necklaces as you see fit."

I take my scarf and put it over my head, making me feel protected in this strength that has been created, and I leave my mala necklace in the crook of my ankles as they have been since they gave them to us. After some moments, Christine says, "Open your eyes and look at your partner, thank her for holding space with you and show her some love."

I look into Liza's eyes, and for the first time, I truly feel connected with her, not just as a member of our best friend group but as Liza. She seems to feel the shift as she gives me a lopsided grin. She speaks, "Thank you for holding space with me. Your energy is so strong and encouraging. I am happy to be your partner."

I reply, "Thank you for holding space with me and allowing me to feel your nurture, care, and strength. I felt like you had me. I am happy you are my partner too." With this, we hug, and the tears begin to flow again. We continue to embrace until the tears subside, which is when Christine says, "Poweress' that concludes this evening's, Sister Circle. Now, you will go to your rooms to steam and begin writing in your journals. I will see you tomorrow morning. Peace." With that, she begins to gather her things to leave.

Liza and I walk out together as we found out our rooms are three doors down from each other.

"Gurl, that was hella intense, like in the best way," I say.

"Absolutely. I don't know what I was expecting, but that was definitely beyond what I could have thought. I still can't believe we both snuck away only to end up together."

"I know, right. Well, this is me. Enjoy your steam."

"You too."

We hug, and off she goes.

Chapter 10: Trina

It's about 3 am, and as relaxed as I am, I can't go to sleep. My yoni steam after the Sister Circle was amazing. It was like because I already felt the connection between God and me, I could hear Him clearer than clear. I was also able to feel and hear my thoughts clearer than clear.

God just kept telling me, "Keep going. Keep going. Don't stop until you hit the point. You will know what that point is. Receive truth."

During my session, I realized many things about why I make the moves I do. I don't trust people. Even when I started thinking about my friends, I only trusted them to a point. Then I think about Jackson. As much as he is my friend, he is not one of the girls, so the bond is different. This thought has me wanting to text him. It's Friday night, so he may be up or out knowing him, and it is only 2 am his time. I think to myself, let's be honest, Trina, you want to talk to him, just text him and see. This retreat is working already. I laugh to myself. Usually, if I feel this way, but we are not together, I don't call him; I just wait until the next day. However, tonight is different. I pick up my phone and text him.

Hey Ja, u up?

I put the phone down and waited to see if I get a response. It takes a few minutes but sure enough.

Na, what u doing up?

I giggle. He always comes back with a Na if I call him Ja. The first time I called him Ja, it was an accident. I just didn't finish his name. Then I was like, that is actually sexy. He thought I was trippin and said if I called him that he would call me Na. So here we are. Truth, I like it, but he doesn't know.

I can't sleep. Can u talk, or u busy?

Busy with what, Na?

I don't know, maybe whom?

Get outta here with that. U know like I do, I haven't brought no one hm in a grip.

Facts. What I don't know is y.

There is a long pause, and I see the three dots blinking. It is almost like he doesn't know what to say. In truth, I don't know why I typed that. Well, actually, yeah, I do, honest retreat and all. The truth is, I really like Jackson a lot. When I look back, I always have. I think that is why I stayed away so long. I know my friends thought it was because they told me not to cause drama since Jackson is Ezekiel's best friend and Ezekiel is married to our best friend, Lyric. But really, I wasn't worried about them. I never am when it comes to men. They just don't get me. Jackson is a whole other beast. Like yeah, brotha is FINE!! Yes, all caps, but it's also the fact that he is intelligent and strong emotionally, physically, and spiritually. He drops random wisdom on me and keeps it moving like he didn't just get all deep, but it is there. He is kind and understanding. He is funny and exciting, and of course, he likes to turn up. Well, and lately, he is extremely intimate. So yeah, Jack has it going on, but why is that giving me pause. We have been doing what we have been doing for like a year, and I don't want it to end. The idea of more is scary, though, and I don't know why. It is almost like I don't feel deserving of the kind of love that would change my life and engulf me. It's almost like I think I am only worth or only allow myself to be worth these meaningless entanglements I put myself in. As all of this stuff is going through my head, my phone rings. It's Jackson. I know without looking because Sex Beat with Usher, Lil Jon, and Ludacris is playing. I take a deep breath and answer.

"Hey," I speak softly. For some reason, I am feeling nervous.

"Are we about to have this conversation over the phone at 3 o'clock in the morning?" His voice is deep, husky, and smooth. The perfect bass and vibration that goes right between my legs. Jackson just makes me want to sit on his face. But that is not what we are talking about.

"I don't know what you mean. It was a simple question. Small talk even." I try and play coy. I should know better, though, because the later it gets, the more straightforward Jack becomes.

"Don't play me, Tri."

"Fine….Well, why haven't you had anyone at your crib in a grip?" Now I have a slight attitude. It's more for defense protection than it is because I am mad. And like always, he reads right through my shit. Kind of like that song Right Thru Me by Nikki Minaj. I play that mug every time I get mad at him for doing just that.

"First of all," I hear him shifting, which means he is probably sitting up now. "Take that attitude out of your voice. Don't be mad because I heard you loud and clear, and you put yourself on blast. Second of all, the truth is…… I don't know why I haven't brought anyone home or gone home with anyone in a minute."

Now I am sitting up. "Come on, Ja, you can do better than that. You don't know?"

"What you want me to say? The only thing I know is that I like having you here more than I think I should. And since you been here, bringing anyone home doesn't feel right."

I take a minute because he is right. This is an in-person conversation, but maybe being on the phone and it being late gives us the courage to have the conversation we have been dodging for months.

"Jackson, if I ask you something, will you be honest with me?"

"Always. Even when you don't like it, you heard?" We both laugh at our inside joke.

"Have you been sleeping with other women since we started fooling around?"

He takes a deep breath and lets out a long sigh. "Truth, once."

"Really? When?"

"Like a couple of weeks after our first time. You and I weren't friends yet, and we had not established us. Remember, it was like a little while after our little rendezvous before we did it again."

"Why do you sound like you feel guilty?'

"Trina, I don't feel guilty, but that question is a little uncomfortable, aright? But like I said, I am not going to lie to you." He is getting testy.

"Jack, you can take some of that bass out. I am sorry I wasn't trying to make you uncomfortable. I am just trying to piece together how we went from just sex to showers, you know?"

He takes another deep breath and sighs. I can imagine him running his hand down his face the way he does when he is feeling anxious. Man, Trina, you know a lot about this dude. I think to myself.

"I want to apologize for breaking our unspoken rules of engagement, but I can't. Trina, the truth is, it felt right. The cuddling did too. At least for me." His voice drops a little at the end. It is almost like he is unsure, maybe even as uncertain as I am.

"I don't want you to apologize."

"Then what do you want? Why are you bringing all of this up when you are miles away? You know if you were at your house, I would have just come over to do this with you."

"Yeah, I know. Honestly, I think the distance is giving me the courage to ask."

"Wait, Katrina Davenport is lacking a little courage." He states mockingly.

"Get outta here with that."

"You know I am messin'. I kind of needed this to happen like this too. I have been thinking about all of this lately and what it means."

"And?"

"Tri, I don't know."

"You don't know, or you not ready?"

"Last week it was both, but after taking some time tonight and talking to Ezekiel and just meditating and talking to God. Now it's more like," he pauses.

I finish, "you are scared."

"Yeah."

"Yeah, me too."

"What you mean?"

"This whole retreat is about being honest, and you know they don't play. It's like you come here to work. You said they got you last time at that Man Power retreat."

"Man, did they? I was like I'm out for the count, and it's Day 1." We both laugh.

"Yeah, tonight was intense. It put me in the place, to be honest with myself. My truth scared me in multiple places, one of them being you."

We stay on the phone breathing. It's like this is the moment. Either one of us is going to jump, or we are just gone keep moving like we didn't have this conversation at all. When Jack starts talking, I think my heart is about to beat out of my chest because, honestly, I don't know what I want to do about this yet.

"Trina, I am falling in love with you." He stops and breaths, but I can tell there is more. "It is messing with me. I haven't done this love thing for a while. Man pause, if this were a movie, Deborah Cox would be singing Nobody's Supposed to be Here right now." We both laugh. "I'm sorry, but for real, that song is how I feel. It's like you are creeping in on me, and I can't stop myself from fallin' or from actually showing you I'm falling. Shit, I sound like a chick, right now." I chuckle to myself. I can tell he is flipping out. It sounds like he is pacing at this point.

"Jackson..." I speak, but it sounds like a plea even to me, but for what? I am not sure.

"Yeah."

"I am falling in love with you too, and it scares me shitless. Cause yeah, nobody is supposed to be this close. You were not supposed to make it this close. This is the reason I only date for three months. But like you said, I couldn't stop even if I wanted to, and when you show me that you are falling, I can't help but fall with you. I didn't stop the shower or the cuddling because it felt right to me. Like so, so right." He has stopped pacing, and he takes deep, slow breaths.

"So now what do we do?"

"I don't know because I don't know if I am truly ready for us to be a real us. You know?"

"Yeah, I do. I feel the same way. It's scary."

"Yeah."

I lay down as I listened to him get resettled. We listen to each other breathe for a while, getting lost in our own thoughts.

I twirl the courage ring I got earlier around my finger for a bit before saying, "Ja?"

"Yeah."

"I was thinking about going to New Orleans when I leave here. I need to talk some things over with my grandmother, but then I think I want to chill for a bit. Will you meet me?"

I can hear the smile in his voice when he says, "You taking me to meet the only person whose opinion actually matters to you?"

"Yeah, something like that."

"Of course, beautiful. How long you going to be there?"

"Maybe the whole week."

"Ok. I have some meetings on Monday and Tuesday. But I should be good to come on Wednesday. Will that be okay, or you need me earlier?"

"No, that works great."

"Katrina. I want you, but I need to make sure I am ready to be who you need me to be."

"I want you too, and I want to be sure of the same." I pause for a minute. "Can we just do what we are doing until we are ready?"

"As long as you ok with the fact that things will keep progressing to something more because I can't stop myself."

"Good. I don't want you to." I look at my bedside clock. "Oh, my Gaud!! Jack, it's 6am. Well, 5 am your time. Don't you have that thing with your Mom's tomorrow? You need to be up and ready in an hour. Why didn't you stop me from talking?"

"We needed to talk. Plus, if you are willing to miss sleep because I am sure you need to be up in an hour too. Then so am I. Us being good is important to me, Na."

"To me too. Thanks for staying on the phone with me. We should get some sleep. Oh, by the way, in the spirit of truth, I actually like it when you call me Na. You are the only one that does."

"I know on both accounts. Good night, Na."

"Good night, Ja." With that, I end the call, set the alarm, and snuggle under my soft sheets. This truth thing is working out already. Jackson feels like I do. One truth out and another to go.

Chapter 11: Trina

My alarm wakes me up at 7a, but of course, I don't get up until 7:30a. I look at the itinerary for Day 2 it says:

Day 2

7a-8a: Breakfast in the Marvel Room

8a-11a: Sister Circle and Workshop

11a-12p: Lunch in the Marvel Room

12:30p-3:30p: Individual sessions with the practitioner in your private room

3:30p-6p: Time alone to relax

6p-8p: Dinner in the Marvel Room

8p-11p: Revealing Sister Circle and end of Day closing

As I lay in my bed looking at the Day's itinerary, I realized 1) I am missing Breakfast, but I need coffee, and 2) This is about to be deep. Just as I swing my legs off the bed, I get a knock at the door. I go to the door, and there is a Starbucks

Bag in front of the door. I pick it up and bring it inside. Then my phone beeps.

GM, Na. Figured u would need that Starbucks just like I needed mine.

I smile to myself as I answer, **Thank you, good looking. Cause you already know.**

Have a good one.

U too.

I open the bag to find my name on the cup with a warm Mocha with two extra pumps of mocha and oat milk and one Splenda. There are also kale and mushroom egg bites. This man pays attention for real. He got my order to a T. Yes, we have been to get coffee together before on numerous occasions, but a Starbucks order and two creams and one sugar are two different kinds of orders.

I send him a smiley face emoji followed by the emoji with blowing kisses. He sends me a smirking emoji and a red heart.

We are in deep water, is what I am thinking when I get a text.

Hey Boo, you, ok?

It's Liza. **Hey yeah, I overslept. Getting ready now.**

Ok, catch u in a sec. U want me to grab u some coffee?

Naw, I'm good drinking some while I get dressed.

That room coffee? Really Ms. Starbucks?

Something like that. I'll see u. Let me get dressed.

K.

I go to the bathroom and handle my hygiene. I apply a little makeup, just enough to pop but be natural. Then I slip on my Savage X push-up and matching thong. I spray on my Aventus for Her by Creed. Then I put on my Ivy Park Knit bodysuit with matching knit jogger. I slide in my Ultra Boost Adidas to match my outfit. I put my phone in my pocket and sip my coffee. Then I open the gift for today.

Inside the beautifully imprinted white tissue paper labeled Day 2 is a pair of Aviators with Poweress written on the right temple. The Aviators are silver with rhinestone accents and black lenses. They are the kind of lenses' where the other person can't see your eyes. They look amazing on me and go with my outfit. I pull out the note that was in the tissue paper, and it reads:

Poweress,

You need to see the truth to walk in the truth. On the tip of your glasses' earpiece, you will find a crystal on the part that will lay against your skin. The crystals were chosen to help you see the truth and walk in it. The Power of Truth can be very bright, but that's why you have shades to walk in that light. Wear these shades and walk in the light of truth.

Peace,

Poweress Committee.

I take off the shades and look in the earpiece, and sure enough, there is amethyst on both sides with the words clarity of all things written inside the temple. I love these gifts. I put my natural waves in a high ponytail. I am not in the mood, nor do I have the time to straighten anything this morning. I check myself out. I look good, good. Looking at the clock I have 2 minutes. I grab my egg bites and eat them on the way to the Relaxation Room.

When I get to the room, I see Liza, and she waves me over. As I walk to her, I realize that everyone is still in pairs. Christine appears and leads us in a group meditation, and then the workshop begins.

****

"Gurl, how was your yoni steam last night?" I ask Liza as I eat my shrimp.

"It was so good. I felt so open with myself. How about you?"

"It was good." I shrug. Liza stares at me for a long time, and then she says.

"Trina, are you going to really share with me?"

"What do you mean? I share with y'all all the time?"

"Yeah, parts of things."

"Well, are you going to share with me? Before you start, not parts of things either."

"Fair. How about we agree to really do this. To be honest and do this process."

"Fine," we both say, and we shake on it.

We eat in silence for a while, and then Liza says, "What if I don't want to be married anymore?" I look up, and she is staring out into the water as we are sitting on the balcony.

"What do you mean?" I speak softly and nonjudgmentally.

"I was thinking last night. I love Dante. I do, but I don't know if our life serves me anymore. I love my kids, but what if I am only a fragment of who I could be without them?" She looks up into my eyes, and I can see the tears forming in the brim of her eyes. She blinks, and one tear falls and then another. I scoot my chair over to her side and bring her into me with one of my arms and wrap the other one around her. I just rock her and think for a long while.

It's crazy because we all think of Liza as the one that has it together, but really, she is just as confused as we are. It is always like marriage is the goal, and it is, but it is not the cure to everything. You still need to be whole alone before you are one with someone else.

I take a breath and then say, "Liza, do you feel like a fragment of you?"

"Yes." She says softly and starts crying again.

"Why?"

She looks up at me like she is asking what do I mean. I say, "Like do you think there is something you should be doing or that you are missing?"

She lays her head down. Then she answers softly, "I feel like I am missing myself. I am always running around doing, but I don't think I do for me. Even just taking this time was a stretch. You know how my planning is and how many things I miss."

"Yeah, but missing you is not because of them. If anything, they can help you with you. They are a part of you." I lift her off my shoulder, so she has to look into my eyes. I wipe her tears and give her the napkin. "Liza, no, you are not the you I knew pre-marriage or even pre-kids. But now, this Liza, I point at her, is smarter, more resilient, wiser, more beautiful than any of the Liza's I have known. Maybe you need to stop trying to get old Liza back and welcome in new Liza. The one who is married and has kids is producing a new bomb-ass beauty line that has me looking like I just walked off the runway with only concealer and lip gloss on." I do a little jig, and she laughs.

"Don't forget those lash extensions you have on that I made too." I flutter my lashes, and we laugh.

"Liza, you are bomb. Maybe it's time you meet the new you and stop running from her." She smiles at me for a long time, and then it turns into a smirk.

"Tri, when you get this wise?"

"Look, I've always been this wise. Yall just don't expect it, so I don't share, and don't be telling my secrets." I push her with my shoulder. She laughs.

"Your secret is safe with me."

"Thanks." With that, we hug, then get up and head our separate ways.

****

During the workshop this morning, they talked about being true to yourself and how in order to do that, you need to be clear on your truth and honest with yourself about that truth. The presenter gave some great pointers on how to stay on that path of truth. One of the things she said is it is essential to take the time regularly, to be honest with yourself. To have medivotion and be honest with ourselves and God about how we feel and what we think, and then really allow Him to help us figure things out.

It was funny because after I steamed and got ready to journal, that is precisely what I did. I was like, God, you brought me here for a reason. What truth am I not receiving, and things just start flowing. I was releasing old anger about my parents, boyfriends, failures. I released anger about the limits I allowed and the limitations I put on myself. It was a lot, and then when it was over, my vision got really clear. It was frightening. As I am thinking about all of this, I am standing on the balcony of my room looking at the water, and I hear a knock. When I open the door, I find my practitioner for my private session.

"Hello, I'm London. I am your practitioner for the individual session." I stick my hand out and shake hers and tell her my name. I notice that she is wearing one of the purple sweaters that all of the Poweress Committee have worn this retreat. I allow her into my room, and she sits on the couch in the sitting area. My hotel room is loft-style, so only a half wall separates the bedroom from the living room. This is where they set up my yoni steam last night. It was beautiful. There was the cedarwood yoni seat smelling amazing and a sandalwood incense burning. The sandalwood mixed with the vanilla scent of the room made my room feel safe and warm. They also sprinkled white roses around the seat. It was a beautiful setup. They laid a Poweress black and purple blanket on the floor across from the center with a note to sit there when the steam was over and use the space to write in your journal. I did, and it was beautiful.

Now the blanket is folded on the edge of the couch, and the room is its familiar warm vanilla scent. London sits next to the blanket, and I sit on the other end of the couch, waiting on her instructions. She smiles at me and then says, "I can feel that you have already started doing the work. Your energy feels amazing. Do you mind if I burn a little lavender incense?"

"That's fine." She pulls out some incense and her incense holder. She lights it and sets it up. Then she turns back to me.

"We are going to start with some deep breaths. I feel your nerves. There is nothing to be nervous about. You already started, and from what I am sensing, it is going pretty good, right?"

I smile at her, "Yeah. I guess so."

We do some deep breaths, and she leads me into a mini-meditation. When we are done, I feel more relaxed and ready for what she decides we should do. Christine told us in the Sister Circle that the practitioners would be intuitive about what we each needed.

"Trina, ask me your questions."

"What if I said I don't have any questions?"

She smiles and says, "I would say you are at a retreat about truth and you are not being truthful."

"Fair enough." I take a deep breath and sigh. "A lot of things came up for me last night. I was able to release a lot of things, but I am not sure what to do about the things I feel I need to change."

"What are those things?"

"Well, my relationship with my friend, my career, my life. Can I really know me, and I live a life without showing the real me majority of the time?" I start twisting my courage ring around my finger. London is waiting for me to continue. She says nothing. "I have worn a mask since I was a child. I could never play like the other children except when I was at my grandmother's house. My parents always wanted me to be prim and proper. I played along for a long time. When I went to college, I wild out in rebellion. Then when I graduated, I realized all of the people I knew didn't know me. Everyone thinks I'm the life of the party, and I am, but I think they all think that is all of me, and it is not. I love silence and intimacy. I love to take a moment and bake. Truthfully, I bake because I haven't danced since I tore my ACL. It's healed and perfectly ready to dance, but I can't. I can go to clubs and dance but not really dance. The kind of dance that embodies my soul and allows me to leap and turn that kind of dance I have not done in years. I used to merge hip hop and jazz and do combinations that had me being picked up by major dance companies in the city, but the problem was my mother wanted me to be a ballet dancer. I don't have the body type for that. Could I have pushed and starved myself to get there? Yes, but I didn't want that. So, I pushed myself the opposite way and tore my ligament. I was laid up and in pain, and all my parents could do was ridicule me for how poor my choices were. With my injury and how it healed, I could never do the jumps needed of a ballet dancer again, at least not full-time. So, my parents ended my dance career and sent me to college for my MBA." I take a breath and wipe the tears. I didn't realize I was crying. The truth is I haven't told anyone this story, not my besties and not Jack. Jack knows I danced but not all of this. I look up and see that London is just waiting. "I want to be me. I want to be free and fluid in myself and what I really want. This jumping from man to man and job to job is not what I want. I realized I do still want my dream from when I was a little girl. I want to get married, have kids, and live a life that brings me joy and laughter and not confusion and ridicule. I live in Houston to get away from my parents, but I am still being rebellious against them. I am about to be 35 years old. Enough is enough. It is time that I actually go for what I want and be who I am. You know?" I arch an eyebrow at her. She just smiles and then replies,

"Yeah, I know. So, what do you want and be honest with me as much as with yourself at this moment?"

I chuckle, and the tears start up again. She hands me some tissue. "I want Jackson to be mine. I want to love him and experience him in a relationship. I want to go into business with Ms. Kathy and take her dance studio to heights she could never dream of. I want to dance whenever I want to, just for the joy it brings my soul. I want to leave commercial real estate, but I want to find the perfect space for a dance studio. I want to live. I want to love, and I want to be loved." I let out a long breath, and then I look up at her.

"Good, because I believe God is ready to do just that for you and with you. I think the service you would benefit from most is reiki. Reiki will help get you aligned and soothed to walk out the truths about what you really desire. Reiki will help push you in the direction, and as long as you go and do what you said and follow God's voice, you will surely manifest all that you stated. Does this sound good to you?"

"Absolutely."

"Before we get started, I would like to tie you with a waist bead, is that ok?

"Yes, please." We stand up, and I have to undo my bodysuit so she can get a good view of my abdomen. I already have three waist beads. One is rose quartz, one is citrine, and the last one is just straight hematite.

"I love that you have our beads. However, these beads are no longer serving you. Would you agree?"

"Yeah. I was thinking about that the other day, how I don't feel like they are doing anything; I just haven't released them yet."

"Would you mind if I release them for you? Since they are ours, we can unlatch them, and you can hold on to them if you need them in the future. What do you say? Are you ready for something new?"

"Absolutely."

"Let's do it then."

She goes about getting her tool and unlatches each waist bead from me. With the release of each one, I feel lighter and lighter. Now there are no beads, and I feel a little naked. I chuckle. London looks up at me and says, "Now let's do the new."

First, she pulls out a waist bead with rhodonite, clear quartz, and hematite. When she lays it across my skin, it feels positively amazing. She tells me that rhodonite will help me make decisions in my relationship and have unconditional love and communication in the relationships I already have. She says it will also help me be in harmony with myself so that I can hold my truths and not begin to fragment myself for others again, not in mind or deed. The clear quartz will keep my mind and inner woman clear, and hematite will keep me grounded. The second bead she puts on me is clear quartz and gold and silver hematite, with a charm that says courage. She said this would keep me clear on the path and stabilized in this new truth, and remind me to have courage. As I look at myself in the mirror, I love them. They are the perfect addition to my current journey. I turn around and hug her and tell her thank you.

We take a little break, and then she has me lay on the couch. She turns on some ocean sounds, and then she begins my reiki session. She starts with breathing, and then she begins the energy massage, which is reiki.

Chapter 12: Jack

I'm on my way to moms studio. She is having yet another fundraising event. I know she wants this studio to work, but she offers lots of free classes, so she is not making much money. I told her she needed a new business plan, but you know moms don't be listening. So here I go again, headed to "volunteer", more like voluntold. I have some Jill Scott coming through the speakers just grooving out. When she starts singing, He Loves Me. It makes me think about Trina. The truth is that conversation last night, well early this morning, caught a brotha off guard. I was going to talk to her when she got back, but I wasn't sure what I wanted to say or do. I knew she was thinking something after the whole intimate shower situation, but I didn't expect her to open the door for the conversation. Trina is good at hiding things, her feelings included. I was just happy that we were both honest last night. It makes me want to just let things flow. That's the reason I agreed to go to New Orleans. Yeah, I met her parents on accident, but her grams is the one who matters most to Trina. Her grams' opinion drives her like none other. I don't think she knows I know that.

I pull up to the studio, and it is full. As soon as I walk in, I see why. I walk up to Mama Lynda and give her a hug and kiss. She leans in, pecks my cheek, and whispers, "Darling, go get yo Mama. She gone be done gave this studio away. We supposed to be selling dinners, her choice not mine, but now she is giving them away."

I drop my head and shake it. I run my hand down my face. "What am I supposed to do? I tried to give her money. She turned me down. Then I offered to be a silent investor and even hook her up with people who know the business. Again, she said no. She keeps saying, 'Dis her business. I need to mind mine.'" I say, mimicking my moms at the end. Mama Lynda laughs because she knows I'm right.

"I don't know Darlin, but I do know that me and Justine are not fit to be the board she needs for this 'business' to take off. She needs new blood she can trust and who respects her." She hands someone else a plate without them paying. "Jack, we need to do something."

"Yes, Ma'am. I'll figure it out. Let me at least see if we can get people paying again." She pats my back as I walk away.

I can't believe moms is giving food away, like what's the point. I get to her as she takes measurements for a little girl's uniform. She has one of the teachers, Michelle; I think it is, with her. Michelle is cute. She has one of those lean bodies from doing ballet. She lacks the kind of curves I like in my woman, but I see she is trying to flirt, so I always play nice.

"Hey, Ladies, how's it going?"

"How's it going? I see you left your po' Moms to fend for herself this mornin', and now you coming in here at 11am, all 4 hours after the fact." I lean in and kiss my moms' cheek, and she tries to swat me away. I keep making kissy-kissy sounds and kissing her cheek. All the ladies are laughing as my moms tries to get me away and play mad. Finally, I bend to pick her up, and she yells, "Uncle, now shoo." We both laugh.

"Sorry, I'm late, Moms. I overslept. I'm here now, though. What you need?" She looks at me and smirks. She tells the little girl goodbye and then looks back at me.

"You remember Michelle right. She teaches ballet. She was just telling me that she has this wedding to attend tomorrow, and she doesn't have a date." I give my moms the evil eye. I can't believe she is about to do this. "So, what you can do is take this gorgeous woman to her cousin's wedding. Right?" I look at Michelle, and she is looking at me like she wants to eat me. I look back at my moms.

"Moms, tomorrow I'm a little..."

She cuts me off, "Jackson Vladimir Anthony, III, don't try to play me, boy. Tomorrow is Sunday, so I know you are not busy." I smirk at her. She is really saying that since I won't go to church with her, I can't be doing anything worth anything. Instead of saying all that, I smirk and say, "Fine, Katherine Desiree Richmond-Anthony. But you didn't have to call out my whole name." She smirks at me as she tries to stand up. It's a running joke between us. When I got old enough to know her whole name, I would always say it back to her when she called out my whole name, within reason, of course. I'm not trying to die. I help her up, and she shoves me on the shoulder.

"Hey, woman, you know you shouldn't be getting low no mo'. I don't think your knees work like that."

"She kicks me. My knees just fine." We are laughing, and then I realize that Michelle is still standing there. Man, this will be a mess. My moms shoves me in her direction. This woman is too much.

I walk up to Michelle and smile nicely, "Hey, I hear you need a date for tomorrow. How about I take you?" She nods. "Ok, send my moms the info and where you want me to pick you up."

"Oh Jackson, thank you so much. This is honestly going to be amazing." She says as she runs her hands down my arm. Her voice is syrupy. You know, like she is trying to dip me in sweetness only so she can drown me later. I remove my arm slowly from the grasp she now has on it.

I smile tightly, "Sure thing." I look at my moms with wide eyes, and she just laughs.

"Yall will have a great time, Jack. Now come over here and help me with this." As we start to walk away, my moms shouts over her shoulder, "Michelle, don't forget to send me the info,"

"Oh, I wouldn't forget it for the world."

I shiver next to my moms as we walk, and she burst out laughing.

"Moms, you wrong for this. I mean, I know you like to get me back, but you know she's feeling me. You see how she is looking at me?"

"Oh, come on, women look at you like all the time. They have since you were 17 and had that growth spurt. I was about to beat a few heffas over my baby."

Chuckling, I respond, "Well, go beat her then."

"Boy, stop it! Michelle is a good woman, and you are not getting any younger. Plus, you don't make all this fuss when Trina looks at you like that." What the hell? When has she seen Trina looking at me like that? I keep looking at the floor because I am pretty sure my face will tell a story I am not trying to talk about with my moms. So, I change the subject.

"What you need help with within your office, Moms. That's where we are going, right?"

"Umm-hmm, you ain't fooling me with that changing topics mess. I see you, baby" I shake my head and open the door for my moms.

****

While we are in moms' office, she has me organizing her stuff. She is overwhelmed with this business, I can tell. My moms has owned many different businesses, but this is the one she always wanted. Now that she has it, she needs help, and she knows it. The problem is she is too stubborn to take it from me.

"Stop looking at me that way, Jack. That is the same way your Father would look at me when I got in over my head." She looks up at me. "You know he used to try and help me too. Make the same kind of offers that you have made me." She sighs, and her voice gets soft, and it cracks. I can take a lot but seeing my moms cry breaks me every time. She does not do it often, but when she does, I break. I wait to speak because I can tell she wants to say more. She hardly ever brings up my dad, so I know there is more. "Jack, this is not like the other times. This is my dream. When I left dancing, I told myself I would come back to it and start a dance studio that would push people forward and give them opportunities that I could not participate in, and here I am, failing again. I just wanted...." She trails off, and the tears are steady flowing. I squatted down in front of her, took the tissues I picked up off her desk and wiped my moms' tears. I kissed both her cheeks and waited for those caramel eyes that looked just like mine to look at me. When she did, I started, "Moms, you are the most amazing and resilient person I know. I know this is hard, even harder than the others, because this is actually what you want to do. I am so proud of you already." She shooed me off.

"No, seriously, I couldn't do what you are doing. I waited until Ezekiel, and I could go into business together, so I had a partner, but you are going at this alone. Moms, I know you want to make this happen on your own, and I know you won't accept me or Eze's money, but I need you to accept help from somewhere. If that means we find silent investors, investors, or even a partner. It would not hurt to partner up with someone. Someone with the same passion as you that may have the contacts that you don't. There are a lot of ways to swing this. Let me know how you want to move forward, and I got you. Moms, you have to do something different. I love you, Moms." I kiss her forehead and stand to leave. I saw in her eyes she heard me, but I also knew she needed time to decide if she would listen to me or not. Before I get too far, she grabs my hand. She gives it a squeeze and then a tug. I look back at her. She smiles at me.

"Thank you, Baby. I hear you."

"That's all I ask." We hug, and I leave her to sit. I tell Mama Lynda goodbye, and then I'm out.

****

I am jamming to Savage by Tank as I take my Sunday run. Contrary to what my moms thinks, I actually go to church on a regular, albeit my regular looks like every other Sunday. I stream sometimes too. I do have a church home, but no one knows that, not even Eze or Trina. It's not a secret, just not something I talk about. I feel like my relationship with God, which is my spirituality, is my business. I am hiding it from moms, though. She would turn it into an interrogation, grilling me every Sunday. She probably would vet my Pastor at that. The idea makes me laugh.

Running is as close to the happiness and peace I feel in the air that I can find on the ground. It helps me reflect, release, process, all of it. Sometimes Eze or Trina comes with me, but today it's just me. As I run, I get a text. Siri tells me it's my moms sending me the info for tonight. Man, I don't want to go, but I don't want to owe my moms either. That shit always backfires. I tell Siri to say ok, and I keep running. I make it back to my apartment and shower. I put on some basketball shorts sans underwear. Yes, I am one of those guys. The ladies don't mind either. Anyway, I pull out a black tailored slim-cut suit with a lavender shirt. They are already pressed. I make sure of that when I pick up my laundry from my cleaners. I pull out some black camouflage velvet loafers. I assess the outfit. I think it will be good. I sit it by the bathroom door. Then I go out in the living room to watch ESPN. I have about 3 hours before I need to get dressed. So, I can pick her up at 6p.

As I watch the game highlights, I start thinking about where I want to move. Houston is so big, and each area has its own feel. I used to want to live in The Woodlands, but that is kind of far from the hanger. I might move out to Katy. Its closer to the hanger, and they are building like crazy. I make a note to tell the realtor to check things out there. I will admit the things she has been sending me are too ostentatious for me. I mean, I have money, but I don't need to have eight bedrooms just because I can. Nor do I want to live in River Oaks and have to stand up for my blackness from all angles. I just want a nice house I can share with my wife and then our kids one day.

That thought still gets me. I used to think I didn't want that. After I watched my pops give up on my moms and leave us. If marriage doesn't make you want to fight, then why do it. I mean, fight to stay. My moms has always been the one to start things, but she can never finish them. It's like she has these fantastic ideas, but she needs someone else to help her walk them out. I think he got tired of trying to help someone who wouldn't take the help, even though they needed it. I get it, but she was his wife. Isn't there some kind of code? I used to worry that I would be just like him, get fed up, and leave my family high and dry. He was just got ghost. I'm sure there are things that moms hasn't said, but at any rate, their situation messed me up on marriage too. But here I am now thinking about a house, marriage, and kids. I shake my head just as my phone beeps.

Hey hot stuff! What u getting into?

Man, Trina is a mess. One thing is always true she makes me smile.

Not much hot girl! U still at the retreat?

Yes, still in Key West. No, the retreat just ended.

Well, was it worth it?

Of course. Always is. I got what I needed.

Which was?

Truth. It's a lot to text so we will have to talk.

Sounds interesting.

What r u doin today?

Man, moms got me goin to a weddiin with that dance teacher Michelle.

There is a long pause. I don't see dots blinking or anything. This makes me sit up. She can't be trippin on Michelle. Come on, Tri, don't be that chick, please. I say to myself. Then there are dots.

Man, you must owe your moms a favor if she did u like that. LOL

Thank God.

LOL nothing and yeah, I was like 4 hours late today.

Lmao. I'm surprised that's all she got you doing.

She made me clean that junky office too

That's bout right. Bet you on time next time.

Shut up, ole' big head girl

Whatever limp dick bastard

DAMN, tell me how you really feel. (Smiley face emoji)

Naw, you r a far cry from that.

Betta be. R u would de-friend me

And you know dis man

That's messed up

U said it. I got to go. Have fun

Not funny

LOL. (Kissy face emoji)

****

I get dressed, leaving the top two buttons undone on my shirt, and spray on some Aventus Cologne by Creed. I look in the mirror and make sure I'm straight. I went to the barber after I left moms yesterday, so I got a fresh edge up, curls got shined, the beard and mustache are lined up, and at the length I like, close to the face but enough length to count. I like my beard in between, not long but not short. Present. Anyway, everything looks good. I grab my wallet and keys and am out the door.

I pull up to one of the new multifamily homes in the Memorial area. I get out and knock on the door. Michelle opens the door, and she looks good in a black dress that hits right below the knee. The dress seems to offer her curves that weren't there yesterday. She may have on one of those contraptions that Trina be talking about, the ones that make the woman's boobs bigger and booty bigger, giving everyone hourglass shapes. I am about to compliment her when she smiles at me, in that syrupy, I will eat you kind of way. I swallow and decide to be a gentleman anyway. After all, she does work for my moms.

"You look nice this evening," I say without the regular extra bass that comes with my compliments.

"Oh, thank you. You look great too. I'm pretty sure you outdressed me."

"Naw, we compliant well. Your black dress and my suit." I give her smile.

She runs her hand down my arm, and I cringe on the inside. It feels weird when she touches me. I don't like it at all. I move to the side so she can walk to my SUV. I open the door for her and then come around.

"Jackson, I love your whip. I would love for us to go to the beach in it."

I don't say anything. Cause I am really like this is the only date. There will not be another.

I turn on some Bruno Mars instead of the Tank I was listening to at first.

As we ride, she talks the whole time, for the entire 45 minutes it takes to get to the venue. She doesn't ask me anything about myself, just tells me about her cousin who is getting married and about herself and all of her dreams for the future. She hints more than once how she is ready to settle down and have a family with a man who can support her how she likes. Honestly, I tune her out after 20 minutes. There is only so much of this I can take.

We get to the venue, a reception hall, and she introduces me to everyone like I am her man. When we get to her parents, her dad is sizing me up.

"Hey Daddy, this is my boyfriend, Jackson. He owns a charter plane business."

"Oh, you are the Jackson we have heard so much about you." Her mother says as she takes my hand and starts shaking. What the hell is going on here? I thought she was showing off in front of her cousins, but she has literally been telling her parents we are dating. Oh, hell naw, it's time to stop this.

"Hello, Ma'am and Sir. I am Jackson, but I am only her date for the evening. Nothing more." I shake her father's hand.

"So, you are one of those friends with benefits kind of men. Is that what you doing with my baby." Her dad gets all in my face with this statement. When I look at Michelle for some assistance, she looks like she is into this whole scene, like I am supposed to fight for her honor. This is an absolute mess.

As much as I am obviously a friends with benefits kind of dude, Trina and my relationship, for example, that is not what this is or their business.

"No, that is not what I am doing with your daughter," I state and step back. "Again, I am only here as her date to this wedding and nothing else."

"So, what about all of the dates yall have had and the fact that you are taking her out of town?"

"I'm sorry, what?" I say and look at Michelle. She looks out into space, just as her mom shows me a doctored picture of Michelle and me at the beach. Her mom tells me to look at the evidence of our love. I scroll, and there are more doctored photos of us at the movie, in the mountains, at concerts. What the hell? I return her phone.

"It was a pleasure meeting you both. I apologize, but I will not be able to stay here tonight. I can assume you can get your daughter home safely. Right?"

"Of course, I will take care of my child since you obviously won't. I told you, Chell, those pretty boy types always break your heart."

"Daddy, don't say that. He may just need to go to work. He does own the place." Well, wow, she can talk, is my first thought. The second is what the fuck, because now her parents are looking at me like I must be leaving to go to work. Naw, that's a wrap.

I look them each in the eye as I say, "I am not with you, Michelle. I have never dated you and will never date you. We are done. Have a good night." With that, I walk to the door. As I wait for the valet, Michelle comes out and grabs my arm. I jerk it away.

"Jackson, we could be perfect together. Don't throw away a good thing."

"Michelle, go back in there with your family. We cannot be anything."

"I love you."

This is getting worse and worse. "Michelle, I don't know you, and I don't like you. I don't want to be with you ever." I am really trying here.

"Jack, it's because you need to taste me first."

"Da Fuck. Look crazy. I'm in love with another woman. She is everything to me, and you don't even compare. She is mine for life, and there is no room for you."

"What you've been cheating on me?" This girl is crazy. I just go with it—anything to get her out of my face.

"Yes. I fell in love, and now it's over." The valet pulls up with my SUV. "It's over, Michelle." She starts to cry, and at least that means she finally gets the point. I am so done with this situation I take my keys and speed off. I call my moms.

"Hey sweets, ain't you supposed to be at the wedding?"

"Oh, the wedding from hell. Bout that you owe me. You home?"

"Yeah, what happened?"

"I'm coming over."

With that, I hang up and head to moms.

Chapter 13: Trina

"Ok, Trina, so spill it. What else is going on? I honestly think the dance studio partnership is a good idea, especially since you are professionally trained and you love it. What else is going on?"

Liza and I decided to share dinner on our last night in Key West. She leaves early in the morning to go home, and I will leave in the afternoon to go to New Orleans.

"Ok, so I have been kinda seeing kinda hanging with someone for like a year now."

"Wait a year? What do you mean, kind of this and that? What is it?"

"I have been in a friends with benefits situation for the past year."

"Oh my. Ok, continue."

"Stop looking so excited."

"Well, you know you don't stay with men long, and even when you tried the 'friend with benefits' thing before, you didn't last but three months."

"I know. I know. But this guy is different. He is all the things and then some." Liza stares at me for a long while.

"Oh, my Gaud, are you in love with him?"

"Truth..." she nods. "I think so."

"This is great. Right?"

"I don't know. I mean, he is one of my best friends now. What if I ruin it like I do all the others?"

"Wait. Stop. Trina, you do not ruin those relationships. Is that really what you think?"

"Yeah," I say softly. She pulls her chair around to me and lifts my chin, so I am looking into her eyes.

"Trina, you don't ruin those relationships. To be honest, you chose relationships that don't last on purpose because you don't want to be vulnerable with anyone. You have these superficial relationships with men. You are not ruining them. You just don't actually want them."

She pauses and looks at me. I twirl my courage ring.

"You are right. but how do I make sure that I am vulnerable with this guy?"

"Tri, if yall are as close as best friends and you have been sleeping together for a year, I am pretty sure you are already vulnerable to him. The fact that you are sitting here worried about it says you are vulnerable. Has he spent the night at your house? In your bed?"

I know why she is asking me this because I don't bring guys home with me, and if I do, they sleep on the couch.

"Truth is he has on multiple occasions…you don't have to say it, I know. But how do I not mess this up if we go there?"

"By never losing the friend part. Being friends first is a major factor. That's why people always say be friends first. As a married woman, I can tell you that your friend tends to give you more grace than your partner. Your friend understands you in a different light. For this guy to understand the friend side and then learn the be your man side, he will be more than capable of understanding, loving, and supporting you. He will see all of you. It's a beautiful thing to be friends first. For now, just ride the wave. Don't rush it, don't overthink it. Just be in it. Agree to stay friends and let things go as they should. Let that man love you. I can see you want to."

She smiles at me. I hug her and say, "You are right. I just need to ride the wave. Agree to stay friends and ride the wave. I deserve a good man who loves me and who I love and respect."

"Absolutely." We laugh.

"You are the best, Liza."

"We already know this" We laugh. "So, are you going to tell me who he is, or is he a secret?"

I sigh. "You have to promise not to trip out. Ok?"

"Ok."

"It's Jackson."

"Like Eze's best friend, Jackson?"

"Yes."

"Oh, my my my. Yass gurl, let that fine man love you." We high-five and burst out laughing.

****

The rest of dinner was chill conversation. I am happy that Liza was here, and I told her that. Truthfully, we never just hang out, just us. This was good for our friendship, and we were what each other needed this weekend. My plane is now landing in New Orleans so I can see my grams.

As I am driving to her house, I get a call. It's Jackson.

"Hey Na. How was the flight?"

"It was ok. You land better."

"I'm sure."

"Why is your mind always in the gutter?" I laugh.

"Sorry, Na, that's you. I was talking about the plane."

"Funny. What's up? I was going to call you once I got to Grams."

"Na, I'm not going to be able to come."

"What, why not?" I whine. I never whine. What is he doing to me?

"One of the pilots got sick, and he was supposed to fly this client to all his international business. The problem is they are taking the new jet, and only this pilot and me and Eze can fly it. With this pilot out sick and Eze having more meetings than me on the books this week and next. I have to go. I am really sorry."

"How long are you going to be gone?"

"About two weeks, maybe 3. This client has meetings all over the place, and there is not enough time in between for me to leave and come back."

I don't say anything. I am really hurt. It's not like we haven't broken plans before, but this feels different. I mean, we can always come to New Orleans for him to meet my grams. He owns planes, for goodness sake. Why am I so sad?

"Baby, please say something. I know this was important to you and, therefore, important to me. I tried everything I could, but nothing worked."

I still say nothing. It hits me. I'm sad because he will be gone for so long. We have gone at max a couple of weeks without seeing each other. If he is gone for three weeks, that will be a month since we have seen each other.

"Baby?"

He called me baby. That warms my heart and wets my panties like nobody's business. I got it bad.

"Ja, I understand."

"But?"

"Truth is, I'm going to miss you a lot. I'm used to seeing you every day. Truthfully. I miss you already, and it has only been a week."

I hear him move around. "Trina, I miss you too. How about I owe you one?"

"How about you promise to be home for my birthday party, no matter what?"

He sighs, "Na, you drive a hard bargain with that no matter what business."

"Well?"

"I will be home for your birthday party no matter what."

"Promise?"

"Promise. You have my word."

"Good because your word is bond."

"You know it, beautiful."

I am in love with this man. Lord help, I say to myself. Then I hear that soft voice, that only God uses, say, "Don't run from it. Rest in it." I smile because God knows I will run.

"Na, you there?"

"Yeah, I'm here. When do you fly out?"

"Tomorrow night. When I was supposed to be with you."

I can hear his disappointment. It makes me feel closer to him for some weird reason.

"Well, please let me know you are leaving and when you land each time."

"I always do."

We are stalling.

"Ja, be safe, ok?"

"Absolutely." He says, mimicking me, and we laugh.

Chapter 14: Jack

I am mad as fuck. Real talk. One of the reasons I own a business is so I don't have to fly like this anymore. I get tired of all the changes and answering to people. Yes, I know I am technically the boss, and it is my plane, but I believe in customer service, which means for all intents and purposes, my money purposes, my client is my boss.

We are back in Paris. First, we were in Italy, Florence to be exact. Then Paris. Then London. Now Paris. I know I need to chill. Eze said the same thing. Actually, he said I sound like I need to get laid. Ezekiel doesn't say stuff like that, but he did 30 minutes ago. This client is needy. I know he is trying to take care of his business, and I am at his beck and call. It's been a week and a half, and he just told me for sure it will be three weeks. I keep trying to say to myself that this is good money in my pocket. It's not working, though. Maybe Eze is right. It has been almost a month since I got any. I know for some people that ain't nothing, but when you are used to that good good every two days tops. It's hard out here for a brotha.

I decided to contact an old friend of mine. He lives in the city. He just hit me back asking if I wanted to roll with him and his boys to a new club that just opened. I haven't answered because I wasn't feeling it, but sitting here doing whatever this is ain't working. I hit him back for the address. I put on a pair of ripped black jeans and a black long sleeve v neck; it's pretty chilly here. Then I put on my dark green combat boots, leaving them untied with my pants inside. I brush my hair back into a bun. Then put on my dark green puff vest with a hood. Lastly, I spray some Aventus cologne, and I'm out. When I get in front of the hotel, I see my Uber is pulling up.

I make it to the club. My boy told me to walk up and give the host my name. She smiles and winks at me as she lets me through. I walk into the club, and the vibe is really nice. There are mirrored ceilings and black walls. The dance floor has lights around the edges and random high-top tables in corners. There are a few booths, but not many. Everyone is dancing. I usually end up at techno clubs with Ant, my boy who hit me up, but this one is straight hip hop and R&B, just my kind of spot. As I make my way to the bar, I text Ant and let him know I'm here. He tells me to get away from the bar and head to VIP. I head to the area with the booths, and Ant comes to dab me up.

"What it do, playboy?"

"Man, you know on that grind. What you doing? Shouldn't you be off recording your next album or something?"

He makes this face like, let's not, "Bruh, that thing is a whole problem. That's why I'm in here. Hopefully, somebody will help me get my mojo back."

"Right, somebody or some booty?"

We both laugh. It has been a long minute since we hung out. I met Ant at a club a while back before he got big in the industry, and now, we still kick it when we are in each other's city.

"Here come the ladies now."

I'm sitting on the couch and drinking whatever brown liquor this is. Just Chillin. These ladies come in, and man, they bad, just like I like. Thick in all the right places, curves you can hold on to. One of the ladies walks my way. She sits down next to me.

"Hey Handsome, mind if I pour myself a drink?"

"Go ahead. Better yet, I could do that for you" I lean forward and look her in the eyes. She has green eyes and chocolate skin. She is gorgeous. It's like nighttime met money, and we are making it rain. Wait, what? How much have I had to drink? I know I was drinking before I left the hotel, and I just had one here. I need to slow down if these are my thoughts. I shake my head to clear my thoughts.

"Well, what I need to do to get you to do that?" She leans forward, exposing more of her cleavage that looks ready to holla at me. She licks her lips. I lick mine in return, and her eyes follow my tongue.

"Nothing much, shorty. Maybe a dance later." I lean forward and start pouring her drink.

"I can do that." She smiles at me and then lets her fingers brush mine as she takes her glass from me. She sticks out her tongue slightly as she drinks from the glass. I shake my head. She is being too easy, and usually, I don't like that, but this whole thing is turning me on for some reason.

"So Handsome, what's your name?"

"You can call me J. What's your name?"

"Tina." Wait, what? I know it's loud in here, but did she say, Trina?

"I'm sorry, can you repeat that?"

"Tina."

I breathe a sigh of relief. Don't ask me why because I am not asking me why. "Kool" is all I say.

She scoots closure to me and puts her hand on my thigh. I put my arm behind her. I lean toward her ear and whisper, "Listen, you seem to be trying to get into something tonight. Am I right?" My voice is low and has all the bass I know women love.

"I'm trying to get something in me tonight."

"Well, what's up then?"

With that, she climbs over my lap and straddles me. I look to my left and right and realize her friends are on the same shit she is on. Then I also realized this VIP section could get private. Walls are protecting us from view, which was not there before. We can still hear the music, but we are in our own private room. She presses some buttons behind me, and our couch gets separated by partitions from the others. I see my boy drop his head back, and the girl drops low. What the entire world is this place? I look at Tina and speak, "So, you do this much?" I smirk at her.

She smirks at me. "Well, I mean, I do own the place. I should know how this goes, right?"

"Do you now?"

"Yeah." She starts to rub on my dick, and he is rising. She whispers in my ear all kinds of provocative things. Sometimes I am down for the talking, and sometimes I am not. It has been a long time since I have been in a situation like this, where there were I don't even know what to call this. The closest I can think of is like the back room of a strip joint. She keeps rubbing and then goes down to her knees. She pulls out my dick, and that dude is ready for action. I let my head fall back on the couch and then feel her warm mouth on my dick. It feels good. She twirls her tongue around, and then I look down, and I see Trina. What the fuck? I blink, and it is Trina who is sucking my dick. My dick is going limp. I stop Tina from sucking, bring her back to my lap, and grind into her. She lifts her dress to give me better access, and she is wet. My man is rising again, so I try and get my wallet to pull out protection, and she tries to hand me one herself. I look at her, and it's Trina. My dick is dead now, not limp but out for the count. What is going on? I am sobered all the way up now.

"I'm sorry Trina, I mean Tina. I can't do this. I got to go." She is looking at me confused, and truth be told, I'm confused too. I mean, Trina ain't my woman. Well, hell, I guess she's my dick's woman. I need to figure this out. I am buckling up pants. I look back to say something, but what do I say. Thank you, but my dick wants someone else.

Thankfully she speaks first. "Don't worry about it. I won't tell anyone. I get paid either way."

What the world? There are so many questions, but you know what, it doesn't matter. I tell her goodbye and wave at my boy. And I leave. I make it outside and decide to walk instead of calling an Uber. That was the weirdest sexual experience I have ever had. Well, kind of. Trina got my dick messed up. I shake my head. I look at the Eiffel tower in the distance. I do wish Trina was here with me. I decided to call her. It's like 3am here, so it's like 8pm there yesterday. She knows I'm in Paris because I texted her when we landed this morning.

The phone is ringing.

"Hey Ja, what are you doing up?" She sounds out of breath.

"Never mind why I'm up; what are you doing?"

"Are you jealous over there?"

"Should I be?" It's crazy for me to have an attitude with her when I was just about to have sex with some chick in a club. I stop and look at the water. I need to get my head right.

"Relax there, killer. I just finished cross-fit at my old gym. My grams takes aerobics here. So, I figured why not."

"You know you Fine regardless."

"Oh yeah. Mr. Jealous."

"Man leave me alone. It's been a rough day?"

She stops whatever she is doing and gets serious, "Is everything ok?"

I sigh, "Yeah. I am just not feeling this job right now. I tried to go out and chill, but that backfired. Now I'm walking alone in the dark."

"It's not dark."

"Ok fine, there is light, but you know what I mean."

"Ja, you sound lonely."

"Stop it."

She pauses. "Grams, I'm over here!"

I hear an older woman say, "Give me one sec gotta go see a man about a horse."

"Oh, my Gaud, Grams."

I can't help but laugh.

"What's her man about a horse?" I ask.

"You don't even want to know." We both laugh.

"Jackson, for real, are you ok? You sound weird?"

"Is that that sexy man you told me about?

"Grams, be quiet."

"Well, shoot, you need to go see that man about his horse?"

"Stop, Grams."

I am dying laughing listening to them go back and forward.

"Hold on, Jack. We are getting in the car."

"K"

I hear Trina help her Grams get in the car, and then she gets in the car. The phone connects to the car.

"Ok, I am back, but you are on the speaker."

I smile.

"Young man, Jackson, right?"

"Yes, Ma'am."

"Oh my, his voice is as fine as his picture."

"Grams, he can hear you."

"Oh, Baby, yo voice sounds like molasses, smooth and deep."

I hear Trina chuckle.

"Thank you," I say.

"Gurl, why you running around here entertaining Theo, who sounds like a scratched record compared to this one."

"Grams!!"

"Oops, I said too much."

"Oh, my Gaud."

"So, Theo, is it?" I ask.

"Please don't encourage this line of conversation, Jack."

"Actually, I'm asking you?" My voice is serious. Usually, I would be playing, but right now, I know I'm not, and based on Trina's softened tone, she knows I'm not either.

"Theo is an ex from back in the day. There is nothing to tell. We had lunch, he sent gifts, I sent most of them back, and he wants another date, but I keep declining. Nothing else."

"Most of them?"

"I have a weakness for a pair of red bottoms. You know this."

"Right."

"Ja, are you mad right now?"

I don't say anything for a moment. Her grandma starts scolding her for messing stuff up.

"Hey, ladies. I am good. I don't have the right to be mad, Tri."

"That doesn't mean you are not, though."

I don't say anything because she is right. I am mad, but like I said, I don't have the right to be. First, I was just where I was. Second, she is not my lady, at least not officially. I can't expect her not to have other options if I haven't made a move. So yeah, I can't say nothing.

Her grams starts talking, "Yall young people hear me, life is too short to be running from what you want. I know sometimes you think you have time, but when you know you want to be with someone, do it. Time will pass, and you will look up and be done missed an opportunity that could have changed your life. Love is a leap of faith, and when you both leap, you can fly. Yall hear me?"

"Yes, Ma'am," we say in unison.

"Now, Jackson, please come get this girl or fly her to you. She is working my nerves. I love you, Trina but baby, you messin up me getting a horse."

We all burst out laughing. They pull into the driveway and tell me bye just as I walk into my hotel room.

Honestly, Trina's grams is right. I need to leap.

I take my shower and start to make my plan. When I get out of the shower, I decide to have devotion. I need guidance. I read a few scriptures, but the one that resonates is from 2 Timothy 1:7 "For God has not given us a spirit of fear, but of power and of love and of a sound mind."

"Stop wavering, Son. Take the leap. It will be worth it." I hear God say.

I take some deep breaths, and I feel a sense of peace wash over me. It's time to leap.

As I am finishing, my phone beeps,

Ja, u up?

Yeah.

Can we talk?

I pick up the phone and call her. She picks up on the first ring.

"Ja, I'm sorry my Grams is crazy. Pay her no mind." She rushes to say.

"Na, she's right, though. Obviously, what we are doing is shifting since jealously is happening."

"Ok, so what are you saying?"

"I'm saying when I get back in a week, we will talk. Naw, better yet, meet me in Paris. We are supposed to be here for four days and then fly to Italy again. You can come to be my copilot for the rest of the trip or return home. Come meet me, Trina, please. I will pay for everything."

"I know you will." I laugh at this woman. "I need to see. I have been gone for a little bit. I need to get back to work."

"Tri, are you dodging me?"

"No. I am leaving here tomorrow to go back to work because my boss has called. I want to come but let me see what I can do. Ok?" She asks softly. It is funny how she can be all attitude and turn up and then get all soft and feminine on a brotha. It messes me up every time.

"Ok. Baby, let me know."

"I will. Now get some rest."

"You too, beautiful."

With that, we hang up. I may need a plan B.

Chapter 15: Trina

Spending the week and a half with my grams was terrific. She is so funny and full of energy. We had some fantastic conversations. It took me about five days before I brought up why I was there. My grams was an Alvin Alley dancer. She was there traveling with them through civil rights and training. She danced until she was about 30 years old. It is crazy because she had my mom and then went back to dancing. Granted, at the time, she and gramps lived in New York, where his family was from. My gramps died when I was ten years old, and I remember that he was midnight blue with pretty teeth. I remember feeling safe when he hugged me and that he was fun to be around. He was always the life of the party, and they had many of those.

My grandfather's family had money from textiles. He imported and exported with the best of them, not illegal stuff. My grams' family had money due to oil on our family property in Louisiana. I always loved to visit my grams and gramps because they made me feel like I could do anything from travel the world to create to dance. I felt free to truly express myself. Even after he was gone, my grams kept that same spirit about her. As I got older, she told me about their love and how they ran away and got married, considering my grams' father was not ok with their dating. It makes sense though my gramps would not pass the brown paper bag test. They moved to Louisiana when my mom decided to go to Spelman in Atlanta. My mom always wanted to find a rich chocolate man to take care of her, so she thought going to school in Atlanta would do that. It actually did since she did meet my dad and married him right after college.

Anyway, I visited my grams after the retreat because I wanted to know how she felt about me finally using some of my inheritance from gramps. Yes, I have lots and live a luxurious life, but the truth is I haven't used any of my trust or inheritance from my gramps. I have been letting it sit. I allow the men I date, the jobs I've had, and my dad to take care of me regularly. I always felt like if I was going to use gramps' money, it needed to be for something important. My shoe fetish is not that important.

As I sit on the plane in my first-class seat, I think about what she said.

"So, Grams, I know you know, I came here for a reason."

"Of course, I do, Baby. But I also knew you would say something when you were ready. Are you ready, Baby?" My

*grams voice is spunky and sweet. It's like a delicious sweet
and sour sauce. It does hold that little shake that all older
ladies have, and her New Orleans accent always makes it
extra saucy.*

"Yes, Ma'am." I take a deep breath. She grabs my hands.

*"Katrina, you have always been able to talk to me. What has
you all twisted?"*

*"Grams, I am ready to take out some of my inheritance from
Gramps."*

*"You don't need me for that, Baby. That has been available
to you for almost ten years." She looks me in the eyes. "Oh,
you mean the big one you have been refusing. That would
mean you have an idea of what you want to do with
yourself."*

*"I want to open a dance studio and use your and my contacts
to get auditions for people in Houston that wouldn't usually
know where to get them. Actually, I want to partner with
someone. Jackson's mom, to be exact. She just opened a
studio, but I know together things would be awesome."*

"That sounds pretty good. Have you talked to her about it?"

*"No, not yet. I told you I usually help her out when I am
home. I think I am just tired of running from my truth. I want*

to teach dance and help little girls fly, just like you helped me. I was a dancer like you, and then I tore my ACL one too many times. Along with the rest of the wear and tear from before."

"Baby, dancing ain't for the faint at heart. I think your idea is great, and if this Kathy is like you've told me about before, then there may be a little bit of convincing needed."

"So, you think it's a good idea and a good way to use the money. I want gramps to be proud of what I use it for. You know?" I look down.

Grams lifts my chin, "Baby, your grandfather would be proud of the woman you have become. He left you that money so that you could take your time and figure out what you wanted without feeling rushed to get married or find a job. He wanted you to live free the way he got too." She smiles and then continues. "I think this idea is wonderful. So much so I would like to invest and be a part of your board if you will have me. If we combine all of our knowledge, I am sure we can put on some performances and host some auditions that will bring out the big wigs."

I jump up and hug her. "Really, Grams!! You putting your money and time in it means you really love it."

"You know I support your choices, but you also know my money only moves when I believe in what's going on. That spark in your eyes says all I need to know to believe you are about to manifest us an amazing studio and opportunity."

We hug for a long time.

That conversation warmed my heart like none other. My grams has always had my back, but that day she showed up for me in a way I never expected. My grams keeps her pocketbook tight. This is a big deal. I breathe. I am so excited. Now I just need to get Ms. Kathy on board and figure out my job situation.

I make it to my apartment at about 9 am. I am to be in the office at 11am. So, I take a quick shower, then put on my lotion and brush my teeth again. I put on some Creed Aventus. I put on a matching bra and thong. I unwrap my hair. I kept it wrapped and put on a hat when I flew this morning. My natural hair is straight and has that bounce I like. Then I put on a black bandage dress and a yellow blazer, some leopards print red bottoms, and my nude YSL bag. I check myself in the mirror, looking ready for work. I grab my briefcase and keys, and out of the door I go. I take the elevator to the parking garage below my building. I walk to my assigned spot and slide into my constellation blue-black pack Jaguar F-type convertible. The roof is up today because

I need my hair to stay straight for work. As I drive, I tell Siri to text Jack.

Hey Ja, I'm back in H-town headed to work.

K, have a good one. Holla at me later.

K.

Then I text my grams and Liza and let them know I am in.

My office is in Memorial, about 20 minutes from my apartment. I pull into the garage, park, and make my way into the building.

"Hey, Sammy!!"

"Hey gorgeous, you've been gone too long. I was missing the view of those legs." I shake my head with a smile and keep walking. Sammy is the building's security guard.

I take the elevator to the seventh floor, which is the top floor of the building. Walking into the office, something feels off. I don't know what, but it does. Melissa, our receptionist, greets me.

"Hey Trina, it's been boring without you."

"Hey, what's going on, Melissa?"

"Gurl, your guess is as good as mine. I can tell you that some really powerful-looking dudes showed up about three days ago and have been going through all of our files."

"Are they cops?'

"Gurl, I don't know, but the bosses are shook. That's why they called you back."

"What do you mean?"

"These dudes started interviewing everybody yesterday, and since you have been making some major sales lately, they need to talk to you."

"Do I need to be worried?"

"I don't know. Honestly, no one who has been interviewed has said anything yet. But it seems really intense."

"Thanks, Gurl."

I head to my office on the right side of the floor. Our offices extend to the right and the left of Melissa's desk. When I get inside my office, I put my briefcase down behind the desk and take a seat. I called my boss's assistant and let him know I had made it in. Within 5 minutes, my boss shows up at my door. This is getting weirder and weirder. He never comes to me. I always have to go to him. I tell him to come in, and he has a seat on one of my midnight blue chairs in front of my desk. He looks at me long and hard. It is making me anxious.

"Victor, spit it out, please. You staring like that is freaking me out." I speak up. We are all on a first-name basis in the office.

"Trina, I am going to give it to you straight. While you were gone, the FBI showed up. They are investigating all the partners due to the possibility of money laundering. They are not sure who or if, but they are talking to all parties involved."

I lean forward on my elbows, resting on my desk. "I'm sorry? All parties involved, what does that have to do with me?"

"Over the past year, you have commissioned over $2 million for the company, which is great, but that is also why they want to talk to you. They are going to talk to everyone who brought in a commission more than $600,000 in the past year, but they are starting with those who brought in at least a $1 million."

"Let me make sure I understand, so all of the people in the office who brought the company more than $600,000 in commission over the last year are now under investigation because someone used this company to clean money. Is this correct?"

"Yes."

"Are lawyers present in these meetings?"

"No, we are offering the interview to the FBI as a part of a good-faith investigation. Your interview is at 3pm."

I stand up. "Victor, let us be clear. I will not attend an interview with the FBI without a lawyer present. Since this company is not issuing lawyers to protect its employees per our contractual agreements, I will acquire my own, and this company will pay their rate period. Seeing as though I now need representation for doing my job and doing it damn well. I will be leaving to find said representation. I will be back for the assigned interview with, again, said representation." With that, I pick up my things and head out.

"Trina, please. Let's not make this a thing. Everyone else just went with it. You are innocent, so there is nothing to worry about."

This white man is confused. I will let him and his white privilege believe what he needs to.

"That may be true, Victor, but that does not work for me. I know better. As I said, I will be back." I walk out of the building and drive down the street and then pull over.

I am freaking out. What in the world!! I pull out my legal card. My father always says you need a lawyer in your back pocket. Because I decided not to return home, my father gave me a legal card for the family's legal firm. When I dial the number on the card, the process starts immediately. I guess it should since we pay them to be on standby. As much as I give my dad a hard about this, I am glad he gave it to me. They assign me a lawyer, and we discuss the particulars. He informs me that another lawyer is headed my way now, and he lets me know he will meet me in 2 hours. I thanked him and sat in the parking lot I pulled over in. I want to cry, but I know I need to call my dad because it's better he hears it from me. I dial the number to his office, and I am placed on hold for 5 minutes. Once he picks up, I tell him what is going on.

After a moment of silence, he says, "And you are innocent, right?"

I catch an attitude quickly, "Excuse me? Are you serious right now?"

"Yes, I am Katrina. I don't know what you are doing in Houston. Yes, we came and saw you, but you obviously have money from other places besides your trust because you haven't touched it in months."

"Right, so I must be up to no good because I haven't used your money or your father's money in a few months?"

"Katrina, it has been six months. You and I both know the way you live requires more than you make. Unless that little boyfriend of yours is fronting the bill. Or maybe there is more. I don't know, so again, I ask, are you innocent?"

"What if I'm not? Then what?"

"I would call the firm and remove them as your lawyers. If you are caught up in something illegal, I will not assist you in evading the law."

"Wow!!" I shake my head, and the tears I have been holding because this situation is overwhelming are streaming down my face. I take off my blazer so I don't mess it up. I am so heated right now. "This is why I don't come to visit you guys. I have been gone for almost ten years because you want to control everything. The first time I call you because I need you, instead of being my dad and making sure I am ok, you ridicule me about a life you know nothing about." I am trying to get it together. I will not break down with him on the phone. How dare he think that I would launder money. "You realize I don't have to steal from anyone. I don't have to do anything illegal. If I wanted to have things easy, I could just take out both my trust and live life. Never having to work a day in my life again, which you hate. Instead, I am trying to figure out my way in the world, and I still can't get support. This is for the birds. I called to let you know the situation. And yes, since you need me to spell it out for you, I am innocent. I brought in all the commission I have and got the promotion I currently have because I worked my ass off, but that's not where you want me to be, so that doesn't matter. Well, you know what, too bad. I am tired of trying to get any love from you guys. You continue to show me there is none unless I do what you think is of utmost importance. Bye, Dad."

I go to hang up, but before I do, he says, "Trina, baby, we love you and only want what's best for you. You could come to use your degree in my office or sell real estate with our firm. You don't have to do it how you are doing it. If you were here, I could protect you and steer you right; out there, I don't know what you are getting into. I love you, honey."

"You may love me, but I am not a little girl that needs protecting. I am almost 35 years old. When will you let me live and not make me feel bad for it? You act like I am out here with five babies and doing nothing. I always have a job, and I always take care of things."

"Well, there was that one time..."

I cut him off, "Are you serious right now? You bring that up, now. I'm done with this conversation." I hang up in his face. I can't believe him. He calls back. I don't answer. Then my mom calls. I don't answer. Then my grandmother on his side calls, and, surprise, I don't answer. I can't believe them. How could he? I am livid and in distress. I want to call my girls, but they are at work, and none of them have ever seen me this way. I call the person I trust most—the phone rings.

"Hey, beautiful, I thought you were at work?"

I start to sob uncontrollably. I can't stop. I just let it out. The frustration from this situation, my relationship with my dad, and the memories from the past that I thought I had dealt with and put away. All of it is washing over me, and I can't stop crying, and sobbing, and shaking.

"Trina!" I hear his despair, but I can't stop crying.

"Katrina, baby, please say something? Do I need to call the cops? Shit, I am too far to get to you. Please talk to me."

I am still sobbing, but I hear he is getting frantic, so I try to calm down some. "No cops. I wish you were here." I start crying again.

"Baby, what is going on? Did someone hurt you?"

"Not today."

"What does that mean, baby? Do I need to call Lyric?"

"No, just you right now. No one hurt me. I'm physically ok." The sobs have stopped, and I am silently crying. "Ja, sing to me. It's the closest I have to your arms. Please."

I hear him tell the taxi to let him out. Then he changes the call to facetime. When I accept, and he sees my face, I see the anger and the compassion and something I can't process right now. He stares into my eyes as the tears fall from my eyes. "Ja, please."

He stops and sits. He looks like he is in a park. Cherry blossoms are falling around him. He starts to sing Kem's "I Can't Stop Loving You," which is one of my closet jams, and he knows it. I listen to his smooth voice sing the words even better than Kem. He is still staring at me. The tears stop as I stare into his eyes. It's like I can feel him in the car with me like the words are wrapping me up in a warm embrace.

He sings, "I can't stop missing you girl. I can't stop feeling you girl. I can't stop thinking about you! I can't stop dreaming about you. I can't stop loving you girl." He looks into my eyes with each line, letting me see how he feels. Allowing me to feel the intensity of what he feels and that last line he usually sings low, which I am usually good with. Today, he sings it just as intensely as the rest, and it is precisely what I need to hear and exactly what I can't process but need all at once. When the song is over, he gives me a sweet smile, and his eyes assess me. I close my eyes and lean my head against my headrest. I pick up a napkin from the cup holder next to me and wipe my face. I am sure I am a mess. I take some deep breaths. I hear him breathing, not rushing me, just waiting for me.

With my eyes still closed, I tell him what is happening at work; I tell him about what Victor said and how I left and called the lawyers. He says nothing, just listens. I tell him I called my dad, and when I get to the part where he asked if I was innocent, I hear Ja take a sharp inhale. I open my eyes and look at him, and he is pissed. I finished the story, and he is seething. He doesn't know what my father was about to say. All he knew was it was out of line. The look on his face says if he and my father were in the same room right now, my father would get bucked all the way up, no questions asked at all. He does not speak when I finish. He has gotten up and started walking at this point. He is no longer looking at me. I can tell he is mad and trying to calm down since that is what I need.

Finally, he gives me those caramel pools he calls eyes. They are calmer and filled with compassion, and I can't bring myself to say what else. "Baby, are you ok?" He says. His voice is deep and smooth like molasses, it's the same voice that usually turns me on, but right now, it is making me feel. I minus well admit this, at least to myself. It is making me feel loved and cared for.

"Kind of. The lawyer will be here in about 45 minutes, so that will be handled."

"And your Dad?" He says slowly.

I look away and take my time. "I think I am done. I can't deal with that anymore. I think I am going to take out my trust and get all of my money held somewhere else. The only reason he knows what is happening is because the family is the lawyers that run it." I take a pause. For the first time in my life, I decided I would admit something that I had never disclosed to anyone but my therapist. I look at Ja, and I think he can tell that what I am about to say will be severe. He takes a seat in a secluded section of the park.

"Do I need to turn off facetime? Better yet, hold on." He pulls out his AirPods and says, "Ok. I didn't want whatever you are about to say to be overheard."

"Thank you." I take a pause. "I have never told anyone this but my therapist. When I was 15 years old, my father raped me." I look away. I hear him breathing. His breathing has escalated. I hear him take a deep breath and exhale slowly. "My boyfriend and I had had sex. It was my first time. When my parents found out, I got into a lot of trouble. That night my father came into my room and said if I was grown enough to have sex, he was ready to show me what a real man was about. It was the worst experience of my life. Well, at least until that point." I look back at him. He has tears in his eyes. I know I do too. I continue. "About two months later, I found out I was pregnant. I was devastated for many reasons. When I told my parents, they were livid, and my mom made an abortion appointment right away. When she left to set it up, My father leaned in and said you weren't even woman enough to use protection. Then he walked out. I went to the room and cried my eyes out. The truth was, my boyfriend and I had used protection, and he didn't actually come inside of me anyway, but my father had not, and he had come inside. So, I knew that the baby I was carrying came from my father. I had no choice but to get an abortion, and my parents and I never talked about it again. My father never came back into my room again because from that night on, I was never in the house alone with him, and my door was always locked. I went to counseling for years, and it took a lot for me to regain myself and know that it was not my fault what happened to my baby or me. I have worked hard to move past all of that and really gain my confidence and self-esteem back." I am crying now, and when I look at Jackson, he is crying too. "Ja, after I am good again and ready to really be the woman God made me to be. When I am starting to walk in my truth, he goes and brings that up. Twenty years later and acted like I was some fast tail little girl getting pregnant. I wasn't. That is the real reason why I left, and I didn't, and I don't go home. Being in that house makes me nauseous, and seeing him makes my skin crawl. I have forgiven him, but I will not and cannot ever forget. I don't trust him. I just learned to hide it. I never said anything because I didn't think my mom would believe me, and if she didn't or blamed me, I think it would break me. So, I have just carried it alone all this time." I wipe the tears from my eyes and look into his eyes.

He wipes his own tears, "Na, you are not alone. You will never be alone again to carry anything. I got you. I mean that. I have always thought you were amazing, and this proves you are more than that. I don't have words for how strong and resilient and all the things." He is talking with such awe in his voice I am stuck. I have never seen him like this. It is genuinely pulling all of my heartstrings.

"Thank you, Ja."

"For what, Baby?"

"For this. All of this is what I needed." I sigh and smile.

"I got you, always."

With that, we say our goodbyes, and I feel lighter. I didn't realize how much holding all of that in really weighed on me. But now, I feel ready to take on the world. I have about 10 minutes before the lawyer arrives, so I do just what I said. I email my lawyer requesting papers to completely remove my contract and trust. I then emailed the lawyer my maternal grandfather used to instill my trust over there and make arrangements for transferring my trust from Davenport & Davenport and creating a new individual contract with him. It is time for me to stand on my own and take care of things myself.

****

When I walk into the meeting with the lawyer, the room gets silent, which is what we expected to happen. My lawyer told me they use these meetings to get information, but the partner who took the money uses it not to support you but to find a scapegoat. Well, that will not be me. We go through all the financials of my projects, and they are surprised at how thorough I am. I remind them that I have an MBA. The truth is, I know what this should look like after they fine-tooth comb every detail of my projects from the last two years. They say I am free to go, but I should not leave the country while the investigation continues. I agree. Then my lawyer and I stand, and I place my letter of resignation on the table, and my lawyer puts down his invoice with the promise that he will sue if it is not paid. With that, I go to my office to get my effects, as my lawyer goes to billing to get his check.

Man, what a day, what a day.

Chapter 16: Jack

We just landed at our last stop. My client is saying that we should be able to fly out tonight. I am so happy because I was about ready to pay Eze from my pocket to handle this. Trina calling me and telling me what she did has me anxious to get to her. Seeing her cry and so vulnerable broke my heart to pieces. It was worse than watching my moms cry, especially since I was all the way out here. I am making sure they refuel us, and we are ready to roll when the client makes it back. My phone starts ringing,

"Hey, Bruh!! How's it going out in Morocco?"

"Pretty good. The client says we may be heading back tonight if his meeting goes well. How are things on your end?"

"Business is good. I closed those two clients."

"That's what I'm talkin' bout. Do you need me to do anything but sign the papers?"

"Naw, that's it. The new clients know you are flying, so they don't expect anything for a week or so."

"Kool. None of this is why you called. What's up?"

"So, you know that I know, and Lyric knows, that you and Tri been kickin it."

"Yeah, y'all the ones that said gon' head and do that." We both laugh.

"Well, Lyric and the girls can't get in touch with Trina. She sent some kind of text canceling her party next week, and all the ladies think somethin' is up."

"So, what you saying is, L asked you to ask me what I know?"

"Don't make it sound so elementary. She is my wife." I think this dude may be whining.

"Dude." I laugh.

"Ok, I know. Well, do you know anything?"

"Naw, we talked, but she didn't say anything about canceling her party."

"Kool." I hear him yell, "He doesn't know what's up."

Lyric yells back, "Tell him thank you."

"Yall, a true trip." I chuckle.

"Shut up. Anyway, if y'all are coming back tonight, we have that business gala with the major business owners in the region in two days. The new business cards are in. You will like them. Did you hear about the fire on Jet 3?"

"The fire? What fire?"

"One of the temp flight attendants dropped the food and set a whole chair on fire. Look, it's in the shop. Hopefully, it will be ready for the summer rush in 2 months."

"Wow. Well, this baby is doing good over here." I say, petting the 737. It really has been nice flying her and having time in the sky. "Alright, I got to go. This is the client. Make sure to text me what hanger we have clear."

With that, we hang up, and the client texts he is wrapping up his meeting and is ready to be airborne in an hour.

****

When I land, I can't get all the checks done quick enough. I head home and shower. I am exhausted. Flying that long was crazy. I start my expresso machine and put on some gray Nike sweats and a matching hoodie sans all things underneath. I spray some new cologne I picked up at a shop in Europe. It's called Baccarat Rouge 540 Extrait. I pull on my black timberlands because they are by the door. Pick up my freshly made expresso and am out the door. It is 3am, but

I don't feel like I can rest until I see her. I know it has been like a day and a half since everything, but the way she looked crying, and all the things she said are etched in my brain. I was supposed to be back in 3 days. I hope she is good with my pop-up. If not, she betta get good. I text my moms, so she knows I made it back safely, but I don't expect an answer.

I jump in the SUV and head to her spot. Once I am there, I park next to her and then decide to shoot a text.

Hey Na, u up? I wait for a beat. Then the dots start to blink. That's my cue to go to the elevator and make my way to her loft.

Yeah. Wyd?

Thinking bout u

I won't lie I wish u were here.

Really?

Yeah.

Then open the door.

Ja stop playing.

I'm not. Open the door.

I hear her running through her apartment. It makes me feel good that she is that excited to get to me. At least I ain't the only one. When she opens the door, I damn near fall. She jumps right into my arms, and her legs wrap around my waist. Her eyes are red-rimmed, and her hair is a mess. She has on her usually short-short pajama sets. I walk into her spot and close and lock the door behind us.

She is cradled into me. I hear her take a strong sniff. I use that.

"What do you think? It's new."

She leans back as I sit on the couch and allow her to straddle me. "That shit is dangerous."

"Yeah?" I smirk.

She smirks back. She takes a pause, and then her expression changes to concern.

"Ja, what are you doing here? I thought you said three more days."

"The client got finished early and was ready to come home. To be honest, I was about to leave him. I needed to get to you and see you. How are you?"

"You ran across the ocean for me?"

"You could say that." I chuckle. "Now, how are you? Your eyes are red, and you have on no scarf." I shoot my eyebrows to her hair. She tries and fails to get that stuff to lay down. I chuckle, and she hits me on the shoulder. I know she is stalling. So, I wait.

"I am good." I arch an eyebrow at her because she expects me to believe that when she looks like this. "Really, I am. I broke ties with my Dad's firm and sent my money to the people who hold my other money. You know my trust."

"I don't, but that is not important. So, you broke ties completely?"

"Yeah. I left my job and hired my own lawyers to stay in my pocket."

"OK, that all sounds like good stuff that needed to happen. Why the canceled party?"

"I don't want to fake in front of everyone else and answer all kinds of questions."

"What do you mean fake?"

"My parents took over my party, and they invited their friends. It turned into one of those birthday parties that are networking opportunities. That is not what I want, and seeing them is not on my list either. I told them that too. I also wasn't trying to see my Grams just yet. I haven't told my

Grams about what happened with my Dad because I am sure she will be ready to kill him or hire someone to do it."

"Me and her both," I say under my breath. She puts her hands on my cheeks and lifts my head, so my eyes are on hers.

"Thank you for everything you have done and been to me this past year. I usually run from relationships, but somehow, you have me as vulnerable as if we were in one. I love you, Jackson. You are the gift I didn't know I needed, but I am so grateful to have." She smiles at me and kisses my cheeks one at a time. Then she kisses my lips nice and soft. I lean back. She sits up.

"Did you just say you love me?" She moves to get up, and I keep her in place. I use one of my hands to make her look at me.

"Yes," She smiles, and I give her a smirk.

"Good because I love you too. There is no way I get jealous over shoes, which you are sending back, then want to kill your pops and fly halfway around the world to get to you in the middle of the night and not love you. Trina, I am so in love with you. My dick even loves you." At that, she burst out laughing.

"Man, I am serious," I tell her what had happened at the club.

"Well, I guess we were both trying to run then." I nod. "Jack, I didn't even bring the shoes with me to Houston. After we talked, I knew I couldn't keep them. I sent them back to him the day I left."

"Good."

She laughs.

I love the sight of her laughing. I want to make her laugh for the rest of my life. I pull her into me and kiss her with all I have. I taste her toothpaste, and then I taste that part that is all her. I let my hands run up her exposed legs and then dip them pass the hem of her shorts and grab her ass. I push up and grind my hips into her, and she moans into my mouth. I pull away.

"Katrina, can I make love to you tonight?" I see her eyes mist and a tear form. If she weren't smiling, I would be worried. I pull out my phone and show her something that I usually never share because I never ask what I am about to.

She looks at my phone, and her eyes go wide. She goes to get her phone and then comes back and settles onto my lap, and shows me the same thing I showed her. It's her clean status.

"Katrina, I know we always use protection before we were together and even together. I want to ask you for something I have never asked or done with another woman before. Can I have you with no sheath tonight?"

She moans, and I swear I feel her dripping on my pants. She nods her head yes.

"No, Baby, I want to hear you. Can I?"

"Yes, Jackson, take me with no sheath," she rubs her hands under my hoodie, and I lift my hands so she can take it off. She moans.

"Fuck, you smell like sex and dessert. I want to lick you, fuck you, and love you all simultaneously. Damn." She says, licking her lips.

I smirk and say, "Then let's do that."

I pick her up and carry her to her room. I remove her clothes, so she is naked before me. I always love how she looks naked. She looks great in clothes, but naked, is definitely my preference. As she lays down, I take off my sweats, and she takes a sharp intake of breath. It's almost like she hasn't seen him before.

I climb into her bed, slowly, gently grazing every inch of her with my tongue. When I get to the apex of her thighs, I open her legs and dive into the most delicious sweetness I have ever had. I suck and lick and then bury my face in her pussy.

She is arching off the bed, and her hand is in my hair. I look up and see that she is looking at me. I then Humm against her. She screams in orgasm. I smile and then continue my ascent. I am hard as a rock, but I want this to be slow. I suck and twirl each of her nipples before I kiss my way up her neck and then settle between her thighs. Before I push in, I say, "Na, keep your eyes on me."

"Ok,"

With that, I push in inch by inch. I can see all the emotions play across her face as she takes me deeper and deeper. I am about burst just from the warmth alone. After I settle entirely in, I feel her contract around me, and it feels like she is bringing me in even further. For the first time, I feel like I can see her soul. I can see her for real, and it is blowing my mind.

"Trina, I love you more than you will ever know." Then I pull out and push in slow all over again.

Chapter 17: Trina

This man is trying to kill me. He keeps pulling out and then coming back in inch by inch, and each time I feel like I am giving him more and more of me. As I look into his eyes and feel each flex of his hips, it feels like he is giving me all of him.

"Jackson, I love you too." It's like me saying that sets him off. He is twirling his hips, and I am meeting him with each stroke. We are going faster and faster, I feel my orgasm rising, and I can see his rising in his eyes. It's like we are in sync.

"I'm about to cum; please don't stop."

"I wouldn't dream of it. Cum with me, Trina."

With that, we cum hard, together. We finally look away as he collapses with his head in the nook of my neck, and I breathe in his new cologne. This is definitely my favorite.

I think I start to doze because the next thing I know, Jack is carrying me to the tub and soaking with me in the bath. We lay there blissfully, taking in the aftermath of what just happened.

Then Jackson's deep, smooth, slightly huskier than normal voice pierces the calm silence.

"Marry Me?"

I move to sit up. He keeps me with my back against him.

"I love you, and I already know you. I also know that I would die for you. I would do anything so that you never look the way that I saw you the other day. I know that I would do everything in my power to keep your beautiful smile on your face. Trina, you are merged into my being. The only co-pilot I want to live this life with. So" He pauses. Then from behind him, he pulls out a box and puts it in my field of vision. This time he allows me to turn around. He looks so confident and sure. He looks like the man I love and trust with all of me. The man I respect and treasure in ways I didn't even know I could. He takes a breath and then smiles. He sits up some and says, "Katrina Marie Davenport, will you marry me?"

A smile forms slowly across my face. He opens the box and takes out the most beautiful black diamond heart-shaped ring circled by blue sapphires and set in platinum. I smile at the ring and say, "Absolutely!"

He puts the ring on my figure and then kisses me like nobody's business, and we go for round two in the tub, with water splashing and moans risings.

Chapter 18: Trina

It has been about two weeks since we got engaged, and we literally have not told anyone. It has been nice just enjoying each other and learning each other as a couple. It is crazy how affectionate Jackson is, something I didn't know. It's like he is always touching me or kissing me, and to be honest, I love it. I usually hate it when a dude is so touchy, but it's like, I crave it with Jackson. It energizes me and makes me feel loved.

I am in his restroom getting dressed for my meeting with Ms. Kathy. I just showered and am putting lotion on my body. I laid out a green bandage dress with a matching wrap jacket and some black pumps, and a black purse with a matching briefcase. My hair is in its natural curly state. I have a little tighter curl pattern than Jack, but it's almost the same as his. When he found out, he loved it. He prefers my hair like this, and to be honest, I think I do too. It reveals the spice that lies inside of me. I part my hair to the side and brush my hair into a tight bun that sits low on my neck. I leave out a few curls at my ears and do my edges just right. Then I go in my Tumi duffle looking for my perfume, and I can't find anything. I go back into the bathroom as I start to freak out. Jackson shows up in the door frame looking so delicious with this mischievous smile on his face.

He pulls a gift bag from behind his back and puts it on the bathroom counter. "You may find something of use in there."

I smile at him. "What are you up to?"

"Open it and find out."

I open the bag and take out one of the boxes. The box is slightly weighted. I open it, and it is my own bottle of Baccarat Rouge 540 the Eau de Parfum version, though. I smile back at him.

He walks up behind me and kisses my ear. "I figured since you love mine. You may love this. It is not as intense as mine. I know you like it a little lighter than that."

I look at him. He is getting sweeter and sweeter. I mouth Thank you as I take the perfume out and spray my pulse points. It smells so divine, and he is right. It smells like his, but just slightly different. I turn around in his arms and say, "What do you think, Ja?"

He leans in and sniffs. His voice is deep and husky, and he wraps his arms around my exposed skin between my high-waisted panty and bra set, "You smell absolutely decadent." He then kisses me slowly and grips my butt just right.

I literally shiver. If I didn't have somewhere to be, I would bend over this sink right now. He leans forward and pulls out the other box in the gift bag. He steps back and hands it to me. I open the box slowly, and it's a pair of beautiful black diamond heart-shaped studs set in the same arrangement and in platinum, just like my engagement ring. They are so beautiful. I smile up at him and then hug him close.

"You are so good to me, thank you."

"Baby, I just wanted you to know I got you, and I support all that you are doing." He leans back, looks into my eyes, and lets his hands rest on my hips. "Katrina, you are about to eat this meeting for breakfast. I have seen you prepare, and I know my moms is a hard sell, but that pitch you presented to me last night had me wanting to invest. Trust me you got this. Go in there and show her you are a boss, and you are ready to take her business to the next level."

I smirk at him, and he pops my butt. He walks out and picks up my dress as I change out my earrings for the new ones. He helps me zip up my dress and leans in and kisses my ear. Then he begins to leave the room. I look at him through the mirror, and I say, "I love you."

He looks at me, "Love you too." Then he leaves me to finish getting dressed.

****

I walk into Jackson's living room, where he is working on his proposal for the biggest client they have ever tried for. If EzeJ gets this client, this will be the cash cow, that client that makes it so that the company goes up in status and the guys really can coast. He looks sexy as his black wire glasses sit on his nose and his eyebrows bunch in concentration. As I walk closer to him, he inhales deeply, and he lets his head fall back.

"Baby, I done messed around and gave you my kryptonite. The way that smells on you got my mind messed up."

I laugh and look into his eyes as I pass his head on the couch, "Well, at least, we are on the same playing field now. When you wear it, I am a goner. So, we are even."

He laughs and stands up. "You look good. You ready?"

I walk into his space, give him a peck, and smile. "Yes. I got this."

"Yes, you do. Let me know how it goes before you get to Label Ladies later."

"You won't be here?"

"Naw, I need to go in and manage some stuff in about an hour. This meeting is in 2 days, so Eze and I need to cross some T's and dot some I's."

"You are going to do amazing. I'm sure of it. The specs look phenomenal."

"Thanks, beautiful."

After another peck, I am out the door and headed to my meeting with Ms. Kathy.

****

Ms. Kathy is at the restaurant. I arranged for us to have a private room for my pitch. We go in, and the room is set with whiteboards and veiled posters, just as I asked. We sit down at the table, and white wine is poured along with water.

"Do you want to order first?" I ask her.

"No, sweets. Let's talk business first."

I dismiss the waiters and tell them to give us an hour. Then I start the pitch. I start with Board 1, telling her her own vision and showing her what she has and where she wants to go. I know this part because I low-key have been helping her anyway. I get to Board 2 and begin to show her the trajectory of income and losses for how the business is going with the current vision. I say to her, "As much as we want to give something away, we can't give it all away." She nods her head because up until now, I haven't presented anything she doesn't already know.

I get to Board 3 and unveil it. There are multiple boards behind it. I see her eyes light up as she takes in the building, dance floors, vaulted ceilings in each dance room, mini-auditorium, offices, audition spaces, and the lobby. I tell her a story as if I am the client walking into start classes. I tell her everything she is offering me, her connections, and the companies and artists that seek out the studio's dancers. I also talk about all the studio's events, including its annual recitals. I end up as the client signing up to start to dance class. At this point, Ms. Kathy is in tears because I have taken her dream and built it past 10.

I get to Board 4 and unveil it. It is just the question of how with a question mark. How can she go from where she is to where I just showed her? She nods like she is following along. I get to Board 5, and there is a picture of me. I begin to tell her what I can offer, from finances both monetary and my accounting skills to the building to connections. She smirks. I recognize it well. She looks just like Jackson when I got him, and he knows it. I continue to Board 6 and show her how a partnership could look. How I would not take over, but we would work together to produce a studio that we can be proud of, and that will go beyond our wildest dreams. I show her how my grandmother has also agreed to invest and be a board member, and I explain how we can have a board for planning and networking. We don't have to go into the public spree and let people buy-in. We can build a dance empire. Then I get to Board 7, and it simply asks any questions.

I look her in the eyes, and she is tearing up. I walk to the table and hand her a tissue. I sit down, and I wait for her. I can see she is thinking.

"Katrina, let me start with that was amazing. I have been in many a board room, and I have never seen a presentation that moved me on all the levels that yours just did. You truly did your homework, and the diligence to detail is amazing."

I don't interrupt her, but it is interesting to see her in her professional self. I am enjoying this dynamic.

"I have two questions, Katrina. One, why me? You could build this without me."

"That's simple. No, I couldn't. We come from two different worlds of dance. We hold two different sets of connections and experiences. It is the merging of those that will take this vision to what I showed you and more."

She smiles. I know it was a great answer.

"Ok, that makes sense. Two, you want us to go 50/50, correct?"

"Yes."

"I started this studio alone because I wanted to do this by myself. Splitting it with you will go against what I envisioned."

"I understand that. The truth is you can tell me, no, and that would be fine." I breathe and ask God to help me. "However, the numbers show you will not make it another year alone. Sometimes God puts a collaboration within grasp so that you can let go of what you thought you wanted and accept the full vision He has for you. We are the body, and we only know in part. But if you take your part and my part and put them together, we have a whole. You will not be giving up on your business or failing because we go 50/50. You will be birthing your business into her greater self. Her God-given self. You have done great. The business has succeeded, people have been coming, but now it is time for greater. The things you want to give for free we will be able to sometimes because of the greater. You have been faithful with little. Now God is trying to give you much and the help He knows you will need with much. The question becomes, are you willing to take it?"

She looks away from me, and she takes a deep breath. She is stalling. I tell her to give me a second. I tell the people we will be back and pay the room off, so they must keep it. I come back in and say, "Ms. Kathy let me take you somewhere." She says ok, and I get my car pulled around.

I can tell she is still thinking because she is not her talkative self. This is a good sign, actually. We pull up in front of a commercial property that I found. I already spoke with the company selling the property, and I have the keys, perks of still having a commercial real estate license.

We get out, and she looks up at the building. I can tell she likes it. The building is white with windows that go down into a diagonal. The windows start high on the left and go down to the corner of the right side of the building, leaving enough white space to place a sign and a design. I unlock the building and show her all the floors and the open spaces.

When we get back to the front lobby, I say, "Now, think about if this building was redone with all the studio pictures I showed you before." She gasps, so I continue. "This place is not too far from the other, and we can keep some of the same furniture and logo pieces you already have. Then I walk to the desk that looks like it was used for a security guard before. She follows. I lean on the desk and say, "What do you think?"

"Honestly, forgive my language, but you a bad bitch." We both burst out laughing. That is the last thing I expected her to say. When she stops laughing, she looks me in my eyes, "Trina, where do I sign?"

I lean over the desk and pull out a brown envelope with a smile, "Right here." I pet the envelope that holds the agreement that would put us into business together.

"See, bad boss bitch." We both laugh, and we hug.

"Now, Ms. Kathy, I am so excited, but I want you to take this to your lawyer and make sure that everything is solid for you. I did my due diligence, but I was always taught to check for yourself."

She smiles at me, "sweets, the fact that you are wearing an engagement ring from my son, is enough to know you got my best interest at heart." She smirks. I look down at the ring and realize she is right. I do have on the ring. I meant to take it off, but it has been on since he put it there, and we haven't really been around anyone, so taking it off hadn't come up.

She sees the shock and worries crossing my face, "Trina, relax. I will act surprised when y'all tell me." I chuckle. "And since you didn't correct my assumption on who gave it to you, I can say it's about time y'all stop running. That love bug bit y'all a long time ago." We both laugh and hug again.

As we walk to the car, she says, "I'm happy he chose you. Y'all are really good together, sweets. Be good to my baby. He is a softy. He is truly affectionate with those he loves. Don't mess him over." She is pointing at me as I hold the door open.

"Yes, Ma'am. I would not dream of it. All I want to do is love and respect him."

"Well, and sleep with him too." She says as she slides into the car, laughing.

I can't do anything but laugh and shake my head—this woman.

We went back to the restaurant and ate. We had a great conversation, and eventually, I got her to agree to take the papers to her lawyer and get back to me in 2 days. In the end, we hugged and left the restaurant.

When I finally get back to Jack's apartment, yes, I now have a key. I finally can do my whole jig and dance it off. I thank God and dance. I then change into my Fendi brown viscose dress and some Fendi boots. Grab my purse and head out for Label Ladies.

Sliding into my jag, I am beyond happy, I call Jackson. He picks up on the first ring.

"And the verdict is?"

"She said yes!!!"

"What, What!! Congratulations, Baby!" He is so excited. Then I hear Eze say, "Baby, huh?"

"Bruh, shut up." I hear Jack get up to move, but before Eze is out of earshot, "So you get all engaged and now you baby dis and baby that." I can't help but laugh as Eze teases him, and then I realize what he said.

"Ja, you told him?"

"Yeah, I didn't have a choice. Dude was all in my business talking about what or who had me glowing and all this other crazy shit."

"It's ok. Your Moms kind of figured it out too. I forgot to take off my ring before the meeting."

"OH, shoot. I need to call her then. It's cool, though. It's not like we are hiding each other anymore, right?"

"Absolutely not hiding, my fine husband-to-be!"

"Say that again that sounded sexy as hell. Claim me."

"Bye, Husband-to-be. I got to go. I'm about to walk into the Gardens."

"Bye, Na. Congrats again!"

"Thanks."

We hang up, and I walk into McGovern Gardens.

The ladies are sitting in our usual spot to the right corner. They have already started eating because I am late.

"Well, look what the cat dragged in," Lyric says as she stands up to hug me. She has on some Fendi combat boots with a scarf. I kiss Erica on the cheek. She has on a Fendi poncho. Then I get to Liza, who stands up and gives me a big hug. She has on a Fendi bomber jacket.

I whisper in Liza's ear, "Hey Boo, how are you?"

She whispers, "Oh, so good. We started counseling!" I lean back and look into her eyes. She has a light twinkling in her eyes—something I haven't seen in a long time. I smile at her and then hug her again and whisper, "I am so happy for you. I guess this truth thing pays off." I raise my hand between us. She gasps and starts jumping. I burst out laughing.

"See, now yall just cruel. Got inside conversations. Like just because me and Erica didn't get to go to the mini-retreat, we can't hear the news." Lyric is being fake salty.

"Oh, Boo, stop trippin. Y'all look good in that Fendi, Yasss!" I say. Label Ladies is really just lunch we ladies have together. We try to do it every quarter to catch up, and since I like a little spice, I said we should all wear the same label so we can be "matchy-matchy." They hated the idea, but they indulged me. So, we call our meetups, Label Ladies. We always come to the Gardens and eat Reggae Hut.

"So, have y'all done the catch-up?" I say as I grab a red stripe.

"You not eating?" That's Erica.

"No, I just had a business lunch. We can talk about me in a minute."

"Oh, no, Honey, we starting with you," Liza states.

I shake my head, and I say fine and tell them about what happened at the retreat in general, keeping confidence as Liza and I agreed, then work and the business meeting between Ms. Kathy and me, and how she agreed.

"Gurl, that is so awesome. I am so happy for you. I knew you would figure it out." Lyric has always believed in me. It is refreshing.

"Oh, no, Honey, let her get to the next part. Continue" Liza is being so messy right now.

"So well, there has been this man in my life for the past year. We have been friends with benefits." I stop. Lyrics eyes are bulging because I told her there is only one way that I would tell anyone. She keeps quiet as she starts jumping in her seat.

Erica is looking at the table, "Wait, so I'm the only one who does not know about this dude?"

"Yes, Boo, I'm sorry. Liza found out at the retreat. Well, and Lyric gave me the green light."

Both ladies give Lyric the evil eye. "Listen, you didn't have to deal with all the sexual tension they were bringing in the house when they would keep the kids or just come hang out. One night the tension was so high it was making me and Eze horny. We were like, look, y'all need to handle this get out."

Everyone laughs.

"Wait, so who is it?" Erica again.

"Oh, my bad, Boo, it's Jackson."

"Gurl Yaasss!" Erica high fives me.

"Let her finish." I look at Liza and shake my head as I laugh.

"Let's just say that things progressed after I was honest with myself, and now" I lift my left hand. "We are engaged."

We all scream and jump up and down. Of course, they ooh and aah over my 4-carat heart-shaped black diamond ring. Then they realize my 2-carat black diamond heart-shaped earrings to match, which sets off a whole other set of screams. We eventually sit down, and they resume eating. Then Liza looks at me,

"Boo, I am so proud of you, and that man looks good on you."

Everyone agrees, and then we begin with the other ladies. Erica goes next. She lets us know her job is still good, and she is still looking for a man. She says she feels a little desperate, and then Liza tells her, "Gurl, stop looking. The more desperate you are, the less likely it is that he is coming. If you stop looking, he will come. Trust me." We all agree.

However, Erica is not feeling it, "I am 37 years old. What am I supposed to do?"

"Let God be God and do what He does," I say under my breath. Liza is next to me.

"I'm sorry. Let God be God, huh. Who are you, and what have you done with our bestie?" Everyone laughs at Liza's joke.

"Leave me alone, ok. Jack has been having me wake up and go to church with him."

"Come through, Jack." Lyric laughs. I give her playful evil eyes.

Erica says, "I know but I thought I found me, and I thought I knew what I wanted."

"That's the problem. You thought you knew what you wanted. God gives you someone you need, and you don't even realize you want." Lyric says.

"Absolutely," me and Liza say.

"So y'all saying just chill out and live my life. When the man comes, he comes. Let God handle it."

"Yup. Trust it is easier said than done, we know. But it will work out." Liza admits.

Erica finishes telling us about the guys she has been out with, and let me just say they suck. Then we move on to Lyric. Lyric has been doing fantastic. She was able to hire a few people to work for her at the marketing firm she owns. Girlfriend is a multi-millionaire in her own right. She and Eze decided they were not having more kids the twins, who are five years old now, are more than enough. She shows us pictures of our babies. We are all their god-mothers. She says marriage is good, and things are moving smoothly most of the time. That last part, she says with an arched eyebrow. Ezekiel is a handful sometimes. I have been there when he is as hyped as the kids. It's kind of funny. Usually, Jack is around. Go figure. Then it is Liza's turn.

"Well, I just finished the new cosmetic line. Everything is scented to smell like different desserts. So, pick the dessert you love, and then the line will have everything you need scented with something of that dessert. Each collection's lipstick and lip gloss taste like that dessert. There is a new foundation that matches you perfectly, making you camera and every day ready while moisturizing, giving SPF protection, and stopping wrinkles. All the lipsticks and lip glosses moisturize and reduce wrinkles, and there are lashes and all the things. Since I know y'all so well, I brought each of y'all a collection." She gives Lyric a caramel truffle, obviously with her Caramel Knight as her husband. She gives Erica a vanilla sugar cookie. We need to spice my Boo up a little bit. Then she gave me a chocolate-dipped German chocolate cake, my favorite cake of all time. I have been trying to make a macaroon that tastes like it. I will get it one of these days.

We all thank her as we try on the lipsticks with that PH system, giving you your perfect shade of pink. These products are bomb, and we tell her. Then Liza gets serious. We wait.

"Also, Dante and I have started therapy, and it has been wonderful. I think I am falling in love with myself and with him all over again." She tells us how she had been feeling and how therapy has helped. We are all so happy for her.

My besties are really the best. We finish up eating dessert and laughing and joking. We take a walk around the Gardens, and then we head out. We hug and set the next date for Label Ladies.

As I drive back to Jackson's to pick up my bag, I decide it is time to call my grams and tell her the truth about everything and about my new developments. I end up sitting in the garage of Jackson's apartment and crying and spilling my guts to her. I tell her about what happened with my father when I was 15. I tell her about the abortion. I tell her about work and how my father decided to bring those things up. I tell her I talked to Jack and how he sang to me and then how I resigned. I tell her about my meeting this morning and about my engagement. The conversation is filled with crying, anger, then more anger, then joy, and love and congratulations.

"Grams, I know I am sharing a lot at once. I just am tired of holding all these things in. I am ready to live in the power of truth, being honest about my feelings with myself and living in my truth. I can't do that if I am not honest with the people closest to me."

"Baby, I wish you would have told me then, but I am happy you can tell me now. I would go bust a few caps in his ass, but it doesn't seem like that is what you want. I am so happy that you are being honest with yourself and that you and that young man finally made things official. Make sure to let him know he needs to bring you to my house so I can meet him. Ok?"

"Yes, Ma'am."

"Now, are you sure that you won't let me at least hire someone to take care of your Father?"

"No, Grams. You are right; I don't want you or any of your goons to shoot him. I just want to move forward in this freedom I have from being honest."

"Well, I understand why you won't tell your Mom, but listen to me, Baby. If you change your mind about letting me handle things, you give me a call."

We both laugh.

"I love you, Grams."

"I love you too, Tri."

We say our goodbyes, and after hanging up, I go up to Jackson's apartment.

Chapter 19: Jack

They got me all the way bucked up. I don't know who these people think they are dealing with, but I think naw. As I am on the phone dealing with the apartment management, Trina walks in the door. When she does, her boots get covered in water. My whole kitchen and living room are flooded. The person next to me had a pipe to burst. When I called the people in the office, they told me they knew and that it was safe for me to stay until they figured it out.

"Listen. I will not be staying here. There is at least a foot of water in this living room. My furniture is destroyed."

"Well, Mr. Anthony, your premium insurance should cover those things. There is no mold, and therefore it is safe to stay. The maintenance should be there sometime on Monday to clean it up,"

"I'm sorry, did you say Monday?"

"Yes, Sir." I mouth to Trina to get her things and pack me a bag. We are about to get out of here.

"I don't know how this luxury apartment expects me to stay in a soaking wet apartment for two days before someone comes to even look at it. By that time, mold would have set in. What I will not be doing is staying here, and I will be sending the regional and national manager an email about the unprofessional and inappropriate way that this situation and conversation has been handled." With that, I hang up the phone. I pay entirely too much for them to think I am going to sit here and wait two days before they come and get this water up. What kind of foolery?

I walk into the bedroom and see that Trina laid out suit options for the week so that I could choose. I love this woman. She picked out some great options, so I started putting them in the suit luggage. I turn and kiss her ear and begin getting things from the drawer.

"I got that stuff already, Jack. All you need is cologne. What is your poison for the week?"

I wink and say, "Aventus and Baccarat."

"My faves." She says as she walks away. I get my work stuff together. At least the bedroom is dry for now because my notes were on the floor. I would have been screwed. I need to make many changes due to some changes the client asks for. I put things in my briefcase and told her to go in the safe and get my items. I don't know when I'm coming home, so I should take my essentials'. She turns back to me as if asking the code.

"8772."

She puts in the code and turns the knob. Inside there is money about $500,000, my rainy day stash. There is also my passport, some jewelry like my Rolexes, and then I know the moment she sees the last thing because she gasps. It's my Beretta M9 pistol and ammunition. She hasn't touched it, which is smart, but the safety is on, so I wasn't worried about it. I come around the bed, kiss her ear and move her over. I put the 9mm in the holster in the small of my back and then packed the rest of the items in the safe. She is staring at me hard. I smirk.

"Is there something you want to say, Na?" I stand up. The safe is now empty, including the files I forgot I had here. The duffels are packed, and she has her things. I look at the room one last time.

Then she says, "Is there something you need to tell me?"

"I don't know what you mean."

"Come on, Jack, money, jewels, passport, and a gun. You looking real suspect right now?"

"You think I'm a drug dealer or something, Baby?"

"Jackson," she whines. As much as I think it is funny, she is actually bugging out about this. I decided to be serious.

I sit, and then I ask her to sit on the bed next to me.

"Na, none of it is probably anything you are thinking. My moms always said to have a rainy day stash that was not in the bank, which is the money. I buy a Rolex for every million-dollar deal we close. It is like my own trophy. When I was younger, I thought that a man with a Rolex was a boss. So, it's how I reward myself. The files are copies of our first deals and the contracts that hold Eze and me together. Then the gun." I run my hand over my face and look out in the distance. I take a beat and say, "Truth is Tri, serving in the Air Force holds some of my best memories and some of the worst. The longer I stayed, the more the worst outweighed the best. So, when I got home, I honestly didn't feel safe without my Beretta. I had been sleeping with one for seven years. It was hard to sleep without one. Once I didn't need it on me to feel secure, I just put it in the safe just in case." I turn back to look into her eyes. Honestly, we never talked about guns, so I didn't know what she would say.

"So, then you feel safe now?" She was concerned.

"Yeah, but I do have a gun at work and in the SUV. They are all concealed and locked away. I need to be able to protect me and mine at all times." She smirked at the last part. "And yes, you are included in my me and mine."

"Ok." That is all she says, and she stands up.

"Are you good with guns? Trina, tell me the truth?" I pull her between my legs.

"As long as they are concealed and locked away, yes. But I will be honest, if we are going to have them in our home, then I would like to know how to use them. So, will you teach me?"

"Gladly. My bad, absolutely." I say, flipping my imaginary hair as she and Lyric does. She pushes me in the chest. I get up, grab our bags and head out.

As we get on the elevator, I ask, "Baby, you don't mind if I stay with you for a week or two until they fix this, do you?"

"Boy, Bye, you don't even have to ask."

"I don't want to overstay my welcome."

"You're welcome hasn't even begun. I planned to be dicked down all week."

We both laugh. I put the bags in my whip, and then I go and help her get into hers. I tell her I will follow her.

****

This presentation is tomorrow, and I am losing my mind. I practiced with Eze over the phone and with Trina in person. I am just anxious. Trina is asleep, and I am pacing in her living room. I walk into the kitchen and find a note.

Relax, Ja. It will be fine. You will do great. Have some macaroons and drink the drink I fixed in the fridge. Then come back to bed. Jackson, you got this. See you soon. Love, Na.

I opened the macaroons container, and sure enough, she had made me my favorite ones, chocolate chip and macadamia nut. She wouldn't let me in the kitchen earlier. Now, I know why. When I open the fridge, there is a bottle of Macallan the Harmony Collection on the shelf and with a glass already poured. I close the fridge and smile. I have wanted to try this particular collection, and I just have not had the time. How she did this when she was at home most of the day with me is beyond me. I take all the macaroons to the couch and sit. I start to eat them. They are so soft and melt in my mouth. I moan out of pure delight. I drink some of my whisky, and the flavors pair perfectly as if she did it on purpose. Oh, this woman. I continue to enjoy the combination. I am relaxing slowly. Then, I feel her presence, but my eyes are still closed, and my head is leaning against a pillow. She doesn't speak, and neither do I. I feel her open my legs and drop down between them. Then I feel her tugging at my shorts. As I lift my hips to help, I open my eyes and look into hers. She smiles sweetly, and then she lowers her head and swallows my man whole. I look into her eyes, and it is like she is saying, I got you. I lean back and let her work, and boy does she. She is holding my base with one hand, playing with my balls with the other, swallowing me, and working her hands simultaneously. I think I have died and gone to heaven. Before I know it, I feel my nut coming. I put down my glass, put my hand in her curly hair, and begin to pump. She lets me take control and bust all down her throat.

When I am done, she looks up at me, straddles me, and asks, "How are you feeling, now?"

I swing back the rest of my drink and pick her up. She is laughing as I carry her to the room to finish what she started.

"Na, you are the best. I love you." With that, I push all the way into her wetness as she screams, "I love you too."

****

Today is the day. I get dressed, gather my things, and head to the meeting. The meeting is early, and considering I kept her up until the wee hours of the morning, I am surprised that Trina woke up and made me my morning energizing shake. I usually make one every morning at my place before work, but she usually is not stocked with all the ingredients here. I guess that is another thing she handled without my knowledge. She tells me I will be fine, and she is praying for me and rooting for me. I kiss her ear, and I am on my way to the meeting.

The meeting goes beyond excellent like they signed on the spot. I literally just landed the biggest contract of my career. I pick up the phone and call Trina,

"Hey Baby, what's the verdict?"

"I just signed them!!" I hear her screaming in the background, and I can't help but laugh.

"Congratulations, Baby!! You did that." I hear the excitement and appreciation in her voice. The sheer love she has shown me the last two days is confirmation I am doing the right thing in making her my wife.

"Alright, Na, I need to call Eze."

"You called me first?" She is getting all emotional.

"Of course, I did. You are my wifey-to-be."

"And you know dis man, Love you, Ja. Call me later. Congrats again."

"Thanks, and I will. Love you."

With that, I hang up and call Eze.

"Alright, what do we need to change?"

"Man, the whole thing," I said somberly.

"Man, but your pitch was on point. What didn't they like? We changed everything they asked for? What they want a whole plane for free or something."

"Basically," I say, trying not to laugh. Bruh is losing his shit.

"Man, you still there? Why you so calm? These fools wasted our time. Shit." I hear him kick the chair and then wince.

"I mean, I guess I'm calm because what will be will be," I pause, "and what will be is they signed the contract on the spot. Bruh, we have just secured the biggest contract of our careers. We can finally breathe."

"Dude, I hate you. We got it for real, though?"

"Absolutely!" We both laugh. Then we do our ritual, and it's my turn. "God, we thank you for all that you have done and are doing with EzeJ. Thank you for allowing us to be brothas and for allowing our friendship to stay intact as we do business. God, we thank you for the opportunity today and for the victory you provided today. Thank you for giving us our hearts' desire and then some. We give you all the glory and all the praise. In Jesus name, Amen."

"Amen. My dude, we need to celebrate."

"Yes, we do. Tell me when and where."

"Let me touch basis with the Mrs., and I will hit you back."

"Bet."

I pull into Trina's apartment garage on cloud 9. It's like everything I could have ever wanted is falling into place. My business is doing well to the point where we will finally be able to take a moment and really enjoy the success. I found the woman who I want to spend the rest of my life with, and she is just as live and as chill as I am. My moms's business is taking off because of my girl. I am in hog heaven.

That is until I get in front of Trina's door and hear yelling and screaming. I used my key and slid in smoothly, not wanting to interrupt whatever was happening so I could get a clear picture before I handled it. What I see has me seeing red in less than a sec. My hand goes to the gun in my back. Her parents are here, and her father has her hemmed up against the wall, and he is grinding into her saying something that has her crying and clawing at his arms. Her mom is standing there looking like Trina deserved what she was getting. I drop my bag. That's when her mother realizes I am standing right behind her. Her father is so enthralled with what he is doing that he doesn't hear me. I roll up behind him, and Trina sees me. The terrified look in her eyes has me throwing ole' dude to the floor and beating his ass. Forget shooting him. He deserves to feel every blow I give him to his face and his body. My hands hurt, and his face is bloody, but I be damn if this dude thinks he is coming up in here assaulting my lady and gone live. Hell Naw!

Then I hear Trina talking very calmly, "Baby, don't kill him. I need you. I love you." Then she repeats it slow and steady, "Baby, don't kill him. I need you. I love you." That is enough to stop my next blow. I honestly don't know how long she has been trying to get through to me, but I am happy she did because I was about to kill this dude. No lie.

I am still sitting on his chest. When I lean in and use all the bass my voice has and all the hate I feel for this nigga, "Motherfucker listen to me clearly, don't you ever step foot in this apartment or our house ever again. Understand, she saved you this time. But there will not be a next time." I pull out my gun and put it to his temple. That is when Trina's mom finally says something.

"Jackson, please, I think he understands." Her voice sends me on a whole other spiral. But I need to finish with him first.

"I will kill you, period. This is not a threat but a promise. I know she let you live and dealt with that shit you did by herself, but she ain't by herself no mo. This" I use my gun to point to his face and chest. "Is only the beginning of what I can and will do if you ever show up where ever we are again. Are we clear?" He nods his head. "This immediately marks the end of any business we have or are currently working on with you. Our contracts are canceled, and if you try and come for me and mine," I push the gun into his skull. "Do you hear me clear?" He nods again. Then I slowly get up, and he takes long, deep breaths. I'm sure I broke some ribs with my weight and punches. He better be happy that's all that's broke.

"Jackson, us staying away is unrealistic, Honey" I snap again and walk into Trina's mom's space. She cowers like I knew she would.

"Listen to me clearly. The only reason I ain't put hands on you is because I was taught not to put my hands on a woman. But you ought to be ashamed of yourself. You just stand there and let your husband assault your daughter."

"It's not the first time." She says softly. I hear Trina gasp and start to sob.

My gun is still in my hand, and I put it to her temple, "The audacity, disrespect, disgust, and slew of other words, what kind of mother are you? She is your daughter. You are supposed to love her."

"I do love her." She moves like she is going to go to Trina. I flick the safety off.

"I wouldn't do that," I say through my teeth.

"Trina, I just wanted to make sure we would both be taken care of for life. He promised it would only be once. I thought you would move on and forget about it. I was securing our future." All I hear is Trina sobbing.

"Get the fuck out, you and your nigga." I point the gun back and forth between them. "If either of you ever come near her again. I will use this without question, and Trina will not be able to save you. Are we clear?"

"You love her that much? You would go to jail for her?" Her father says as his wife helps him up, and they go toward the door.

"I would die for her. I will protect her, love her, and support her until the day I die. Something the two of you failed to do."

They are standing in the hall now. I hear Trina behind me. I can't bring myself to look at her yet. She comes in front of me with tears in her voice, "I loved you both, even after everything. I tried. But you guys never did and never will. I no longer want any parts this." She points between herself and her parents. "We are done forever."

"Trina," her parents say in unison.

Trina cuts them off with a raised hand. Her voice is now calm and confident, "No. We are done forever—no calls, no texts, no visits, no following me. And when I marry this man behind me, no you will not get invited, and when I have his children, you will never, and I do mean never see them. If you choose to break any of this and show up, I will not try to save you. Jack will be free to do what he deems necessary like today." She shakes her head no. "No more. I will not try because you no longer exist." With that, she closes the door in their faces and locks both locks.

She waits for a few beats. I put the safety back on and put the gun back in my holster. I wait. When she finally turns around, I see the dried tears and makeup on her shirt. Then I look into her eyes, and I expect to see hurt or even anger at them and me. But, what I see is love and resolve. I put my arms out to hug her. I'm not sure how much she wants to be touched right now, but she immediately jumps into my arms and wraps her legs around me.

"Baby, I am so sorry I wasn't here."

"You were right on time. You saved me. You are my safe place. Thank you for standing up for me."

"You don't have to thank me for that. Thank you for not interfering with how I was handling things but letting me stand up for you how I know how."

"You would have killed him. Wouldn't you?"

I sit on the couch, "Truth, yes, I will do what I need to do to protect me and mine, and you are mine. Can you be good with that?"

She leans back and looks at me. I wipe the tears that are falling. Then she replies, "Yes, as long as you love me, protect me, and support me forever and always."

"I can do that. I will need you to love me and respect me forever and always."

"I can do that."

We stare into each other's eyes, knowing that as long as we stay like this open and honest with each other, the sky is the limit. The power of truth is astonishing because the truth really did set us free.

The End.

Epilogue: Trina

One year later

"It is truly my pleasure to be the one to present the Business Achiever of the Year Award tonight. The awardee is my brother from another mother. He is my best friend, my children's godfather, and my business partner. He has shown what it takes to shoot for the stars …..."

Eze is talking, but I zone out as I look at my fine husband, looking as delicious as he smells. He feels my eyes because he looks at me without turning his head. He gives me his arm and pulls me closer.

This past year has been busy and fulfilling. We got married six months ago in a destination wedding that included my girls, Eze, Grams, Ms. Lynda, the twins, and Mama Kathy. Ms. Kathy insists now I am her daughter, so Mama Kathy only. I love it. The wedding was all I could ever want. The sunset on the ocean with the people who love us most as we said I do before God. I will never forget how he stared into my eyes and revealed his soul as he gave his written vows. After the wedding, we had a bomb reception, of course. We drank and danced the night away. It was beautiful and exhilarating.

After being married for three months, I had Jackson fire his realtor because she was doing a horrible job. I took over and found us a house near Lyric and Eze but not in the same subdivision. I love our home. It should be done being built in another month. I can't wait. Every time we visit, it swells my heart. Jackson has been having us go in and pray over the house at every stage, from ground to foundation to walls to paint. It has been excellent. It feels like God has already blessed our home with peace.

Mama Kathy and I are doing really well. We finally agreed on what all the rooms needed, and renovations started on the building a few months ago. Now we are picking color schemes and lining up teachers and events. Michelle will not be working there. In fact, she no longer works for the studio at all, after what happened. While all the renovations were going on, we started running the current studio together, and I have been teaching some classes. I love the feel of being in the studio and allowing my body to take over as it wants to. For the first time in my adult life, I feel like I am right where I am supposed to be.

"Please give a round of applause for this year's Business Achiever of the Year, Jackson Vladimir Anthony, III." Ezekiel finishes.

Jackson looks at me and smiles. I give him a peck, and he stands up, buttons his midnight blue tailored suit, and kisses his moms's cheeks. Then he walks to the front. We are all screaming. The twins are screaming, "Go, Uncle Jackson!!" It is so cute. I look at Lyric, who is across the table, and we give each other that knowing smile, life is good. My grams bumps my shoulder. Jackson flew to New Orleans yesterday to pick her up for tonight.

I look her way, "Are you ready?"

"No time like today, right?"

"Exactly." We both laugh.

I listen to Jackson give his acceptance speech. He talks about things in his life and thanks all the people who helped him. He thanks his moms for all of her sacrifices, encouragement, and love. Then he talks about Ezekiel, and it almost brought me to tears. Mama Kathy started crying and had to reach out for my hand.

"Seriously, Eze, I don't think we would have made it this far without you. This award is as much yours as it is mine. You have made me a better businessman, man, and husband. I am truly grateful for our friendship and our partnership." With that, he reaches out to Eze, who is still on the stage. He dabs him up, and then they give each other a real hug. All the ladies, ooh and aah. Then my tears finally fall. Their brotherly love is one you always like to see because black men don't always show that. I love that they do. They release each other. Jack dabs his eyes, and then he makes eye contact with me.

"Oh, here it comes," Grams whispers and pats my knee. Mama Kathy squeezes my hand.

"And to my beautiful wife. The moment I met you, I knew I needed to have you. It took some time, but we finally got it together." He smirks at me, and I smile. "Every day waking up to you makes me want to go harder, reach higher, be better. Every time you encourage me, support me, let me get all sensitive," everyone laughs, "and respect me leading us and trusting I got you makes me want to give you all I have physically, mentally, emotionally, and spiritually. Giving you my name was the greatest achievement of my life. Thank you for loving me when I'm wildin' and when I'm chillin and when I boss up. Thank you for appreciating me and showing it daily. Thank you, Katrina Anthony, for being you. You are all I could ever want and dream of. God gave me the best gift in giving me you. I love you, Baby." I am a ball of happy tears. This man and his words get me every time. I yell, "I love you too, Baby." Everyone laughs. My grams leans over and says, "That a girl." Then I laugh too.

Jackson has to stay in the front for pictures and networking. I stand up, and Mama Kathy nods towards Lyric. I nod back. We decided earlier in the week to use Lyric's company for marketing the new studio, so I walk over to her and say, "Excuse me, Mrs. Thompson, can we discuss some business this week? We would love it if you would be our marketing agency for the new studio."

Lyric jumps up. "Gurl, stop playing. I would love to. Let's meet Wednesday. We can do business and then lunch. Have your people call my people, Mrs. Anthony." Then she hands me a card, and we laugh.

"Seriously, I am calling."

"I know."

"Auntie Tri, you look so pretty. You match Uncle Jack." That is Lyric and Eze's daughter Am.

"You think? Is that kool?"

"Absolutely," she says and then flips her hair. I give her a high-five like I do the girls and then look at Lyric. We fall out laughing.

Erica comes over to our table. "Hey, y'all. This event is super nice. I have made some contacts."

"What kind of contacts?" I say suggestively.

"Maybe a little of both." She pauses. "Oh, my Gaud!" Lyric and I turn to see what Erica is looking at, and Oh my, Gaud, is right. Lyric and I both cover our mouths.

Liza just walked in late, first of all. She is always on time. Then she shows up looking like pure sex. She has on a silver mermaid dress that is corseted and hangs on her voluptuous body like a glove and then flares giving you hints of flirtatiousness. Girlfriend's hair hangs long down her back when she usually has it pulled tight into a bun. But this is the kicker, she walked in with this fine chocolate, and I mean, deep chocolate dove dark chocolate brotha, with a freshly shaped full beard and mustache, fresh edge up, with the most beautiful black and slightly highlighted blonde locs that are wrapped in a design that leaves some locs hanging. What I am saying is brotha is fine fine. Yes, I know I am married, but my eyes are not dead. Liza and this dark chocolate man are matching with his black tux and silver chain and silver stud earrings. They look absolutely delicious, and they are headed to us.

I feel Jackson roll up behind me, actually, I smelt him before I felt him.

"Ladies, do we need to be concerned?"

"My question exactly." That is Eze. He is behind Lyric.

I finally tear my eyes away from Liza and turn around in my man's arms. "Never."

"Then why are you staring so hard, Na?"

"That's Dante!"

Both men step back and look and then look at us. Lyric and I say in unison and nodding.

"Yes, as in Liza's husband, Dante LeBlanc!"

They are now looking as shocked as we are. Liza has not brought Dante to anything in years. Like, I haven't even seen him. They finally make it to us.

"Hey, Boos!" Liza says as she lets go of her husband's hand to hug us. Then she turns to Jackson and says, "Congratulations, Jack!! This is amazing."

"Thanks, Sis." He looks toward Dante and arches and brow. Dante is waiting patiently. He is still patient and smooth. Liza turns and gives him the most seductive smile.

"I can't take it no mo" Jackson laughs at me. "Dante!"

"What's up, Tri!!" I go and give him a hug. "It's been way too long."

All the ladies say, "Absolutely!" The men shake their heads.

Liza introduces the men to Dante, and the men start talking. We pull Liza to the side.

"Boo, Oh my Gaud!! First, you look sexy as hell!" I say.

"Gurl, that dress makes you look like Liza pre-kids. Like we going to club and you and Dante sneak off kind of Liza." Lyric says.

"So, you brought the Hubby…." Erica trails off. Liza laughs at all of our antics.

"Yes, I brought the Hubby. We are good, y'all, like really good. When I tell you, I feel like Liza pre-kids but matured by kids and found a new 2.0 kind of sexy. I mean all of that." She snaps her fingers.

We all say, "Yaaassss!!!!!"

"Boo, I am so happy for you, and Hubby looks good."

"Thanks, I saw y'all staring." She turns to look his way, and he winks at her. When I say swoon-worthy, I mean that. "He is mine all mine, and I have no plans of letting that go."

We all smile and hug her. It has been too long since we have seen this, Liza.

After we small talk for a bit, the girls go see the kids, and I walk up to the guys. "Do yall mind of I still this one, real quick?"

"Not at all, do you. "Ezekiel says. I grab Jackson's hand. He follows me into the corner. I stop by the table to get a gift bag.

When we get to the corner, I start with, "Congratulations, Baby, you deserve all the things."

He is looking at me with smiling eyes. "Thank you."

"What you said was amazing." He gets closer and pulls me into him using my waist.

"I meant every word." He leans in and gives me a passionate kiss that would have led us to places if we had not been in public, but we have time for that later. I pull back, and he looks at me curiously. He squeezes my butt before he releases me. I put the gift bag between us.

"I wanted to give you a little something to say congratulations." He looks at me and then takes the bag. I begin to twirl my courage ring from the retreat.

"You didn't have to do anything."

"I know, just open it."

He moves the blue tissue paper to the side and then pulls out the small rectangular box. He hands me the bag. Then he looks up at me with a smirk. Then he opens the box. His eyes go wide.

"Na, are you serious right now?"

I smile wide, "Yes, Ja, we are having a baby!!"

"We are having a baby?" His eyes are wide with excitement, and he looks down at my stomach and then back at me. There are tears in his eyes. "We are having a baby!"

"Yeah, Baby" I dab his tears and hug him close. He pulls me tight.

"So, we are happy, right?" I ask.

"Absolutely." He answers with a smile.

"I love you, Jackson Anthony, forever and always."

"I love you too, Katrina Anthony, forever and always."

Note from the Author

Thank you for taking this journey with me as we watched Trina and Jackson's love and growth unfold. It was truly remarkable to write this and see how Trina and Liza bonded during the retreat. I pray that you found moments of laughter, love, and passion as you read this. I also pray that you took a moment to see some of your own truth and begin to live in the Power of Truth. It is a journey, and sometimes we fall, but the beauty is that God is always there to pick us up, dust us off, and lead us on. Take your journey.

Please lookout for the next book in the series, Power of Honesty, Liza and Dante's story.

Peace and Love, Minniel

P.S. If you are interested in experiencing the beauty and clarity of Medivotion or the healing and revelation of Reiki or if you need a Life Coach to help walk out the words God has already planted within you, please go to my website www.peacebeloved.co and book a session. I look forward to taking the journey of Poweress with you.